T0193402

Follow Me Still:
In the Beginning

WENDY LITWINSKI

authorHOUSE®

AuthorHouse™
1663 Liberty Drive
Bloomington, IN 47403
www.authorhouse.com
Phone: 833-262-8899

Published by AuthorHouse 08/21/2023

ISBN: 979-8-8230-1268-3 (sc)
ISBN: 979-8-8230-1269-0 (hc)
ISBN: 979-8-8230-1267-6 (e)

Library of Congress Control Number: 2023914573

Print information available on the last page.

Contents

Acknowledgment

Jessica, Monica, and Kate, my best friends, you've known me at my best and at my worst; thank you for your prayers and friendship. Pastor Eleanor, you've been a great blessing to me as both a teacher and spiritual mother; thank you for helping me be free. Finally, thank you to my son, Thomas. We've been through a lot together; I love you times infinity.

Chapter 1
A New Beginning

The Lord thy God in the midst of thee is mighty; he will
save, He will rejoice over thee with joy; he will rest in his
love, he will joy over thee with singing.
—Zephaniah 3:17 KJV

"I'll race you to the apple tree!" I yelled the challenge to my son, John.
"You're on," he said, smiling as he took off running full speed ahead,
the tents he was carrying flapping in the wind.

He beat me. *Of course he did*, I thought. He always did. John was six
foot three and had long, muscular legs. I am five foot five with shorter,
thinner legs. By the time I got there, he was already sitting on the ground
with his back to the apple tree, staring up into the clear blue sky. The long,
hot days of summer were becoming a little shorter and cooler, and soon
fall would come, bringing (she hoped) a bountiful harvest.

"What do you want me to do with these green tents?" John asked.

"Same thing I did with those plum trees," I said, nodding toward the
trees. "See how I tied the tents to the longest branches to create a net to
catch the fruit."

"Yes," John said. "But why?"

"To make sure all the fruit is edible," I replied. "If it falls to the ground
in our absence, it will rot."

"That makes sense," he said. "I think the birds, squirrels, raccoons, and opossums will leave the fruit alone. Do you think we will have enough food this winter?" John asked stoically.

"Yes, we sure will," I prophesied. "We will have more than enough."

"Good," he said with a smile as he stood up and got to work on the first apple tree.

It's so quiet, I thought. Not even a bird was chirping. The wind blew gently through my long blonde hair, causing my lips some grief and reminding me that I would need a haircut soon.

I leaned against the eldest pear tree and marveled at my son's maturity. Then it came over me: *They are coming. Go back home.*

"Hey, John," I said, "where are the dogs?"

"Sleeping on the porch. I wore them out playing fetch."

"I'm sure you did," I said, shaking my head.

"Race you back?" he asked excitedly.

"I can't." I sighed. "I'm exhausted. I've been gardening all morning."

"You plant stalker!" John teased. Then, suddenly turning serious, he scolded: "You need to eat more."

"Well, I did eat some young plums," I replied. "They taste sweet—just like candy."

We began the long walk back. The trees had been planted well to the south of the house by design. A vast kaleidoscope of blue butterflies flittered in the sun's rays and lighted on the wildflowers under our feet. The sun had begun to inch its way down, signaling the end of another late-summer day.

I had always wanted the world to change, to get better, but no, this was a hundred steps back from our peak in the year 2020 when we had hope, new technology, so much promise, so many dreams.

"Mom," John said, interrupting my thoughts, "I'm worried about you."

"No need," I told him, swatting the air. "I'm fine."

"Fine?" John wasn't convinced. "You lost a lot of weight, Mom, and I checked—you're almost out of thyroid medicine."

"Going through my stuff again, eh?" I said, raising an eyebrow and cocking my head. "I only lost eighty pounds these last two years. I weighed myself this morning. At one hundred forty pounds, I am average weight for the first time in my adult life. You've never seen me at an average weight.

Look, my hair is thicker, blonder, and longer." I struck a pose. "I'm healthy. Thank you for your concern, but please don't worry."

"Easy for you to s—"

"God said they would be here soon," I stated confidently. "And I'll search for more medicine when they come."

"Who are you talking about, Mom?"

"I'm not sure. I sent out twenty letters three months before the Fates took over. God always tells me *in part*. We will see soon enough," I assured him.

As we approached the house, I saw all five of our dogs lounging on the porch in the shade. *Must be nice to be able to lounge around all day*, I thought as I sat down on the wooden rocker.

You can rest too. It's a gift I give freely to My children. You must receive it.

"Want a glass of water?" John asked.

"Yes, please," I replied. "That would be lovely."

Feeling suddenly exhausted, I closed my eyes and drifted off into a deep sleep.

"Wake up, Mom!" John whispered, shaking my shoulder. "Here's your water, Mom."

I jolted awake. "What?" My tone was sharper than I intended, and I glared at him for disturbing my peaceful sleep.

"Lookee." John pointed toward the five dogs, all of which were focused intently on the timber-and-stacked-stone main entrance. "Brody's hackles are standing straight up." He squinted and scanned the wooden gate and beyond. "The gate's still latched, but do you think the Fates found us?" His voice was strained. "Should we hide?"

The truth was that I couldn't say for sure. "Did you check the security cameras?" I asked, rising from the rocker.

John shook his head. "No."

"Why not?" I asked.

"I thought I'd wake you first," John replied.

"Okay, but next time, check the cameras first."

"Sure, Mom," he said. "I will."

"Anyway, look, Brody's tail is wagging. He knows whoever is on the other side. He wants to play with them."

"So that's good, Mom, right?"

"Could be," I said, heading down the steps and out toward the main gate with some apprehension.

The dogs followed closely behind John and me, sniffing the air, except for Brody, who began to bark with a full-body wiggle, excited.

"Who's there?" I shouted.

A long moment later, a man's voice replied, "It's Mike, Sarah, and the kids. We've come to seek shelter."

Relief. I smiled. "What verse have you read today?"

In one voice, they shouted, "Zephaniah 3:17!"

"All right, good." I unlatched the gate. "Come on in!"

Before they all scrambled in, I put my right arm up and said, "Wait. Mike, Sarah—hold out your right forearms and show me."

"Yes, of course," Mike said, nodding.

Mike rolled up his shirt sleeve and extended his right arm toward me, palm up.

I held his fingertips and searched intently for a small scar.

"Right there," Mike said, "just up from my wrist. See?"

"Yes," I said, inspecting the three-inch-long scar on his forearm.

"We cut the microchips out and left them at home in a bucket of water," Mike assured me. "And we never chipped the kids, because they were under eighteen."

"Me too," Sarah said, holding out her forearm so I could inspect her scar.

"So far, so good," I said. "Let's go in." I nodded toward the house, hoping Sarah wouldn't lie to me this time.

It will be okay, Lilly. Trust me.

Where's Rebekah?" I asked, noting that she was the only one of their five children who was not with them.

"Oh, she's not with us anymore," Sarah replied cryptically.

"As in …? She's still alive, I ho—"

"Yes," Sarah said. "Sorry, not the best choice of words. As far as we know, yes, Rebekah is still alive. She left home on her eighteenth birthday, right before the world changed. We haven't seen her since."

Trying to change the subject, Mike interjected, "Where's the fountain of youth, Lilly?"

"The fountain?" I said.

"Yes," Mike said, smiling. "You still look so young, Lilly. How did you manage to turn back time?"

I shrugged. "What do you mean?"

"Well, we're all pushing forty," he explained, "and though Sarah and I look our age, you still look like you're in your twenties."

"You're too kind," I said with a shrug. "It's just that God blessed my entire family on both sides with baby faces. Thank you for noticing." I nodded toward the house, motioning them to follow me.

Sarah approached John and gave him a side hug. "My, my, John, you look so mature. Look at all those muscles. How tall are you now?"

"About six feet two, I think," he said, face a bit flushed. He smiled at me shyly. "The muscles are from all the hard work Mom has me do. Keeps me in excellent shape." John smiled coyly as he ducked out and walked over to the kids.

Following John, Brody ran up to the kids and barked excitedly to request attention from each of the guests.

The four kids looked older; in fact, I didn't really recognize any of them. We had wasted so much time angry at each other over trivial stuff—stuff that should have made no difference to any of us.

"He looks like Scooby Doo!" seven-year-old Clair exclaimed while petting Brody.

"Sort of," I said. "But he's a shepherd/pit mix or a shepherd/boxer mix. Scooby looks more like a Great Dane, and he's afraid of everything. Not Brody. He's fearless. Well, he's only scared of certain things, like swinging bats, bags, and brooms! He's also a little smarter than Scooby."

That was true. Brody was the smartest, funniest dog I'd ever had, and I was hopeful he would live many more years.

"Down, boy!" I commanded Brody.

"It's okay," Sarah said, stroking Brody's back. He had jumped up on her again and draped his front paws over her shoulders, head bowed against her forehead in submission, tail wagging. "I see Brody is getting gray around his muzzle. Has it been that log since we've seen you?"

"It's been five years," I said tersely, wondering how she could forget that day—the day I felt so angry and sad and alone and betrayed by the people I had grudgingly let in at God's request. "So that makes Brody fifteen."

"And who do we have here?" Sarah asked, motioning toward the other dogs playing with the children.

It was clear she was trying to steer the conversation away from all that had led to their five-year estrangement. I went with it, said, "The white German shepherd is named Fire, and her mate, the black German shepherd standing beside her, is named Ice. The blue tuxedo pit bulls are named Thing One and Thing Two. The pit bulls are a little over two years old, and the shepherds are six."

"How cute!" Sarah exclaimed.

"I like their names," Mike said, nodding. "What do they mean?"

"Well, white-colored fire is the hottest and most dangerous. And we all know that black ice is a lethal threat to drivers in the winter here in Michigan. Fire and Ice are both whistle-trained guard dogs. See how the shepherds hesitate just a bit? Since they don't know you, they won't approach you until I give them the okay."

"Wow," Mike said.

"Watch," I said. I waved my hand toward the kids and blew the dog whistle around my neck. Immediately, Fire and Ice ran up to the kids, jumping, barking, wagging their tails, and licking their little outstretched hands. "I'll never regret the several thousand dollars I paid to have them trained at a police K-9 school when they were just puppies before the world ... well, before everything changed."

"Yes," Mike said, shaking his head. "Before everything changed."

I paused for a moment and watched John approach the children and give them a big hug. They hadn't seen each other in five years. Despite their current situation, the little ones seemed happy. *That was a blessing*, I thought.

"And the other two dogs?" Mike said.

"Ah, yes, as for Thing One and Thing Two, I always wanted a pair of pit bulls from the same litter—twins. Hence the names, with a nod to Dr. Seuss and *The Cat in the Hat*. John used to love that book, so he helped name those two."

"Wow!" Sarah exclaimed as we walked toward the house. "This place is amazing. Why didn't you say anything to us?"

"Well, I did, five years ago," I replied. "You wrote me off as crazy—as some sort of a doomsday nut."

Sarah didn't reply, just stared off into the distance to avoid a confrontation, as she so often did.

Mike spoke up. "We never said you were crazy. We simply didn't believe the world would change. You saw the little changes that no one else could see."

"Or *would* see," I corrected.

Mike squinted and just looked at me for a long moment before smiling and changing the subject. "So are you going to show us around?"

"Of course," I said. "Come on; follow me." I began walking toward the greenhouse, which was directly behind the main house. The daylight had begun to fade, and everyone followed, including the dogs. "When John and I first moved here to Clare in middle Michigan, the house did not have solar power, but it did have a well and a massive generator. God told me to convert from gas and electricity to alternative energy sources immediately. I hired workers to fence off an acre of panels on the south side of the property, in front of the fruit trees. Everyone in town called me crazy, too: 'doomsday prepper' and 'paranoid prophetess of doom' are just a couple of the nicer things they called me."

"Well, it turns out you weren't the crazy one," Mike said.

I shrugged. "I just followed what God told me to do anyway. I had the entire sixty acres enclosed with a ten-foot-tall privacy fence and built a ten-acre hydroponic greenhouse directly behind the main house equipped with solar panels and a backup battery system. The plants rely on salmon and whitefish to provide them with nutrients. Eventually, when the fish population increases, we can eat some of them, too."

"Yum," Kyle, the eight-year-old, said.

"We've got all kinds of fruits, vegetables, citrus trees, and two large beehives in the back of the greenhouse. The citrus and coffee trees span the entire greenhouse between the two beehives. The coffee tree is only four years old and bears no fruit with beans. The barn behind the greenhouse is where the dogs stay most of the time when they are not with us. The barn also stores all the gardening equipment and a smoker. Behind the barn, there is a small seasonal garden with root vegetables, pumpkins, squash, corn, and watermelon. The barn and greenhouse are electrically heated and hooked up to an alternate solar battery system. Hidden security cameras in the house, barns, and fencing help alert us to any strangers lurking outside."

"This is really impressive," Mike said. "Just incredible."

"I was just obeying the Lord," I said. "Now, look back and to your left. We have a variety of trees: apple, pear, plum, and peach. We should have fruit this fall. Surrounding the fence line are blackberries, blueberries, raspberries, and strawberries."

"Yummy!" It was seven-year-old Clair's turn. The kids all gazed intently at the fruit trees, though none was yet bearing any fruit.

"Sounds like you all are hungry," I said, thinking they looked hungry, too. "Come inside the house so we can eat." I opened the sliding glass door and motioned them all inside.

Before passing through the door, I stopped and looked at Mike. "So do you and Sarah have any idea where Rebekah is?"

He sighed and lowered his voice. "Rebekah moved to California when she turned eighteen, not long before the world changed." He couldn't hide his sadness. "We haven't heard from her in three years."

"I'm so sorry," I said. "Don't lose hope. Maybe Rebekah will make her way back home."

"Perhaps," Mike said, trying to force a smile but sounding doubtful; then he turned to walk inside.

Mike, Sarah, and the four kids sat down at the pinewood table in the kitchen, eager for a good meal. As John began setting the table with cups, bowls, and silverware, I rummaged through the fridge and gathered kidney beans, lettuce, tomatoes, and the last few oranges.

As I served the food, I realized the children must not have eaten a square meal in weeks, maybe months. All four were very pale and thin, accentuating their blue eyes and long blond hair in dire need of a cut.

As I began filling their cups with water from the sink, Elise, their sixteen-year-old daughter, exclaimed, "Wow, you have running water?"

"We sure do," I said. "The well was dug brand-new for the house."

Mike nodded. "About those solar panels on the house, barn, and greenhouse … I am surprised they can supply enough energy for heat and light in the winter. How is that even possible in Michigan?"

"Each building has its own independent backup solar battery system. The fenced-in solar panels feed into the greenhouse to produce energy for the aquaponic pumps and provide heat in the winter. The house and barn have geothermal heating in the winter. We only watch one hour of movies on Sunday after Bible study. The lights remain off during the day and on for one hour a night in the winter. We do not use lights in the summer. One well supplies water to the house, the greenhouse, and the barn. Therefore, the shower schedule is limited to one day a week. We are on city sewage, but we have run out of toiletries other than bar soap and toilet paper."

"How on earth did you learn how to design such a place?" Mike asked.

"I didn't," I admitted.

Sarah looked puzzled. "Then, how—?"

"God told me what to do," I said. "Step by step, and I followed."

Mike just looked down at his food and said nothing. *In five years*, I thought, *not much has changed*. Mike still doubted that I heard from God. After everything that had happened over the past two years, I marveled at how anyone could doubt God's hand in this.

Clair, the seven-year-old, broke the silence. "Can we eat now?" She was the youngest and still extraordinarily impatient and somewhat wild. I remembered how as a young child she would race after the boys, climbing over couches and up onto the counters with no fear. Still, I couldn't help thinking something had changed in her.

"Let's pray first," Mike said. "Father God, thank You for this food and for those who listen to Your word. Bless our fellowship and this glorious food. In Jesus's name, amen."

"Amen," we all echoed.

We all ate quickly and cleaned up the kitchen together. I was glad for the extra help cleaning up, as I had begun to grow weary.

Eight-year-old Kyle said, "I'm tired. I want to go to bed."

"Come on," I replied. "I'll show you the bedrooms and the rest of the house."

Everyone followed as I guided the tour.

"The white door to your right leads to the garage; the white door to your left leads to the basement. Straight down this hallway from the kitchen is the living room. The white door past the stairs in the living room is to a bathroom. These wooden stairs lead to the bedrooms and more bathrooms."

I led the way up the staircase. "Here is a loft space your entire family will share." At the top of the stairs, I opened the glass doors to the ample loft space, which was furnished with a king-size bed, three sets of bunk beds, a small sofa, and an old, dark oak dresser.

"I get the top bunk by the window." Jeremy, their eldest son at seventeen, climbed up and lay down on the bed. Kyle and Clair claimed the other two top bunks, while Sarah and Mike settled down onto the king-size bed. Elise stood silent, surveying the room and beyond.

"Ms. Lilly," Elise whispered politely, "could I have the room between John's and the bathroom?"

"Don't be rude!" Sarah chided.

I looked at Sarah. "It's okay for her to ask." Then I turned to Elise, who was looking down in shame as she padded over to the lower bunk against the left wall, which looked out toward the hallway. "Elise, dear, another family will come soon, and they'll need the room."

Elise didn't respond, just nodded faintly. She lay down quietly on the bottom bunk, closing her eyes as all the children did. I noted that Elise had grown quieter in the last few years and seemed to radiate maturity, which I had not seen in her previously.

"Mike, there are extra sheets in the dresser," I said. "You can cover these glass-paned doors if you like."

"Okay," he replied. "We are all tired, so I will figure it out tomorrow. Good night, Lilly."

"Good night all," John and I responded while closing the loft door behind us.

As I reached my bedroom in the far hallway, I realized John had followed me. He said, "Mom, do you think the children will be okay? They all look sick."

"Yes, they just need rest and some food," I assured him. "You will see. Pray for them." I hugged him. "I need to sleep now, and you should too."

"Mom, is it okay if I stay up for a while? I want to check on the fish and gather some extra food for breakfast."

"That is a *great* idea. Be sure to check the citrus trees, and bring in any oranges and lemons you find. Keep the walkie with you, and take Ice. I love you." I walked into my bedroom.

"I love you, too," John said while quietly walking down the stairs.

*   *   *

I awoke several hours later to the comforting sound of children's voices coming from the kitchen. I threw on some blue jeans and a T-shirt and hurried downstairs.

"Good morning," I said, cheerfully.

They were all seated at the table, eating berries and oranges. The dogs sat beside the children, eagerly anticipating any unwanted food.

"Morning," Sarah and Mike said between bites.

John looked up from his bowl. "What's on the agenda today, Mom?"

"Did anyone feed the dogs?" I asked.

"I did, Mom," John replied.

"Well, the rest of the chores on the chart will need to be completed," I said. "I had us weeding, picking berries, composting, and worm hunting. Since there are more of us now, we will need to decide who does what."

"Worm hunting sounds like a job for us guys," Jeremy said, and Kyle nodded.

"Hey, I want to hunt worms too!" Clair shouted.

"That was easy," I said. "Any takers for berry picking? It includes washing, canning, and freezing."

"We'll do it," John volunteered. "I'll show Elise the process." Elise nodded.

"That leaves composting and weeding," I said. "What would you like to do, Sarah?"

"I'll weed," she said.

"Perfect," I said, "and I'll compost. Mike, I have a different job for you. I need you to figure out how to take materials from the neighboring houses' barns and create a fence that will join us with the houses."

"Okay," Mike said. "I can do that."

"There's more," I said with a wink. "It would also be great to add more living space to the house. I have a desk you can use to draw up plans in the basement."

Mike shook his head. "Well, that will take more than a day."

"I know, but by winter you should be able to have a feasible design and plan in place. We will all help build. Others will be joining us soon, and we will need more space. Now let's get to work," I said, as I pulled the compost container from the cupboard below the kitchen sink.

Everyone got up, washed their dishes, and went outside, except Mike. He went downstairs shaking his head and muttering something under his breath about this being impossible.

"How many worms should we collect?"

"Thousands!" I told him. "We need to feed the fish for a week!"

Jeremy nodded. "And where do we look for them?"

"I'll show them where the jars are," John said. "Come on; I'll show you the best spot to dig for worms and how to wash them properly."

Jeremy and Kyle followed him outside, while Sarah and I walked out back to the compost bin behind the barn in silence.

"Where do you want me to weed?" Sarah asked.

"Between the rows of berries spanning the left-side fence, between the rows in the outdoor garden, and around the ground trees in the greenhouse. We weed one fence side a day, twice a month. Put the weeds in a bag and bring them back to the compost bin. The brown bags and gardening gloves are inside the greenhouse in the metal container to the right of the door."

"Do I need to lay down any compost?" Sarah asked.

"Not today," I said. "Next week, the chores list will include laying down compost, and we'll do it again in the fall after the outdoor garden is plowed under for winter."

"I got it," Sarah replied before disappearing into the greenhouse.

I had ended up with the quickest, easiest chore. On the way to the compost bin, I picked up all the dog poop I could see. I got to the compost bin, dumped in the waste and poop, churned the container for a few minutes, and walked back to the main house. As I approached the house, all five dogs ran excitedly past me. They were chasing each other, butterflies, birds, and insects. I smiled, shaking my head at them. It must be nice not to have to worry about anything.

You don't, Lilly. I will take care of you. Have faith. More help is coming.

Part of me knows that, I thought. Take this from me.

The twins are your cross to bear. You must find them. You must succeed.

All right, I whispered. Please help me be strong. Comfort me. Give me grace. Walk with me now.

I walked inside slowly, got a cup of water, and sat on the couch.

"I know," I said. "God, grant me more faith. Please help me not to worry. I've been so tired and overwhelmed lately. Heal my body."

You will need to leave tonight, after dinner. You will have a short time frame to find more medicine. Rest now. Others will arrive to help while you are gone.

"Thank You, Lord, we need a lot of help," I whispered while laying my head down on the soft couch pillow and falling quickly into a deep sleep.

I awoke several hours later to some big, wet sloppy kisses on my face. "Brody, stop now!" His entire body wiggled as he punched at the couch cushions, barking with excitement. When that didn't wake me, he licked my face and jumped on and off the couch. Someone had let him in, and now he needed to go out again.

"All right, come on!" I commanded as I slowly sat up and rose from the couch.

I opened the door, and he quickly pushed me aside, stepping on my left foot as always as he ran out to greet the other dogs. I closed the door, shaking my head. I must have missed lunch, which was fine. I wasn't hungry anyway, as I had become accustomed to eating once a day. The house was silent, and I figured everyone was outside finishing up their chores. I turned to go upstairs to pack when the back sliding glass door opened.

"Hey there," Sarah said. "You're finally up. How are you feeling?"

"I'm okay," I replied groggily, "just a bit tired."

"Are you sick?" she asked.

"No, it's just that I am running out of thyroid medicine, and I've been skipping every other day."

"Oh," she said.

I lowered my voice. "Please don't mention it to John, because he will worry about me. Now that you all are here, I will leave tonight to find more medicine."

"Do you want Mike to go with you, Lilly? I can ask him, but I'm sure he won't mind. It's dangerous to go alone." Sarah laid her hand on my arm, genuinely concerned.

"Thank you, Sarah," I said. "I really appreciate your concern, but no, God told me to go alone tonight. He will protect me."

"All right," she said. "I came in to get dinner ready. Want to help?" She set a bag of fruits and vegetables on the granite counter.

"I really should go and pack," I replied, and I turned to go upstairs to my room.

I figured Sarah or Mike would try to talk me out of going, and that was not a conversation I was looking forward to having with either of them at this moment. As I walked into my room, I heard everyone enter the kitchen. They seemed to be discussing me, although I couldn't make out what everyone was saying. *Oh well*, I thought, *they will just have to accept it*. I had no other options left. I had to go now. As I was deciding what I needed to pack, my bedroom door suddenly flew open.

"Mom, no," John said. "Sarah told me you are going. You can't leave! It's not safe! You might die!" John was frantic and desperate to change my mind.

"I am going, John," I said sternly. "I will leave tonight. You know I need more medicine. God told me to go *now*. He will protect me. End of discussion."

"But Mom," John pleaded, "last time we went to town, somebody shot at you. How are you going to make it back alive?"

I shrugged. "That bullet only grazed my shoulder. The wound healed beautifully. We made it out and lived to talk about it—right now, in fact."

"I will come with you," he said, "since there's nothing to fear."

"No, you will stay here," I commanded. "This farm is your legacy. You need to step up and start leading now."

Then I turned my back to him and began to pull clothes out of my dresser and lay them methodically on the queen-size bed, saying nothing more.

"Mom!" John shouted. "Talk to me, please."

I spun around and looked him in the eye. "Listen, John, you are eighteen. I know you are trying to protect me, and I appreciate it, but I need you to stay here with Mike, Sarah, and the kids. I won't be going into town. I'll try some of the smaller pharmacies and cabins north of here. I only have one month of thyroid medicine left."

He lowered his head and stared down at the floor.

"Son, I trust you to be my eyes and prepare for winter while I am gone. Mike and Sarah have not been through a winter with us. You need to teach them and the newcomers how to prepare for it. I don't want to have another winter like year one."

"Yeah, that was pretty rough," he agreed. "But Mom, I don't want to stay here. I am older now. I can hunt and protect you. I am sure Mr. Mike will follow the instructions you left in the blue binder in the kitchen. He is an intelligent man. So what do you say?" John pleaded, still trying to change my mind.

Brody had entered my room with John and lay on my bed, moaning as he often did when we argued. "Brody agrees with me," John said. "See."

"Stop," I said, turning to pet the beast. "It's okay, pretty baby, I'll be okay. You stay here with John and help out as you can." Brody sat up straight and stared at me, tail wagging, stripe standing up, wanting to play. Brody's dark brown eyes seemed to stare into my soul. I stared back, which prompted him to turn his head sideways and point his ears, as big German shepherds often do.

Brody stared at me stoically, then began wagging his tail. "RRRRRufff!" We often described him as being fifty-five pounds of crazy.

"I love my sweet boy," I said softly as I stroked his back. "Settle down." Brody immediately jumped off the bed and disappeared underneath it—no small feat for a medium-sized dog.

"Mom, you are not listening to me," John said, exasperated. "You are playing with Brody!"

"Enough. I heard every word you said. Bottom line: I need you to stay here. Feed the dogs and get everyone ready for dinner. I need to pack. Prepare Ice; he is coming with me."

"But Mom—"

"Is that the third or the fourth 'but Mom' in this conversation?"

"Probably fourth," John said. "But Ice is my favorite dog. Why don't you take Fire or Thing One or Thing Two?"

"You already know the answer to that question. Ice will blend into the darkness of night. I need him to be my eyes and ears," I explained.

"Good point," John said, the battle over. "I will do as you say. I have a surprise for you before you leave." He turned and walked quietly out of my bedroom, closing the door behind him.

*   *   *

Finally, peace. I pulled my large brown hiking backpack out of the closet. I had gotten it at a camping store before the world began changing. It was already filled with necessary supplies for survival—matches, a metal water bottle with a filter for river water, dehydrated food, a metal bowl, a knife, a loaded handgun with some extra rounds, and a blanket.

Nowadays we had to always be ready to run. People were either indifferent, evil, or gone. Mass disappearances occurred two years ago when the power grid went down, taking our modern forms of communication with it. With no more internet, TV, or cell phones, we resorted to long-range CB radios, which had declined in use since the seventies as truckers began to use more technical, internet based ways to communicate.

John and I had survived out here on our own for two years. Nobody had come until Mike and Sarah showed up yesterday, exhausted and hungry, with their four kids in tow. I knew John wanted to protect me, but I could not put his life in danger anymore because I needed thyroid medicine to survive.

I'd had my thyroid removed over twenty years ago and was dependent upon a daily dose of medicine to provide the missing hormones my body no longer produced. I had about four weeks' supply left, and our farm was at least a week's walk from any stores or pharmacies. Unfortunately, we no longer had a vehicle or even a bike, and all the horses from the surrounding farms had disappeared. I could only hope the horses had managed to escape and run wild instead of being captured by the Fates.

I continued packing, adding a map, a journal, some pens, solar-powered walkies, and the solar-powered contraption that enabled me to listen to *Thru the Bible* sermons. I would have to add more food and water for Ice and myself after dinner. I sank into the soft red rocking recliner, and instantly my mind felt at ease. I usually sat in this recliner and prayed multiple times a day. Sunlight shone brightly enough through my bedroom window to illuminate my entire bedroom, casting gentle shadows on the midnight-blue walls.

Thank You, Jesus, for telling me to move here six years ago.

Oddly enough, we had not had any hostiles or friendlies since year one. True, we were far from any major city and on Clare's northern edge, just barely within the town limits. It was just so strange how one day a group of radicals—who called themselves "the Fates"—took over the town. The power grid shut down, and then people and animals started disappearing or turning up dead.

I picked up the older iPod and earbuds and smiled, thinking I would need it for entertainment since Ice was not a very good conversationalist.

A knock sounded at the door. "It's Mike. May I come in?"

"Sure, come on in. What's up?"

"Well, John and Sarah told me you are going out by yourself to look for medication. In this … day and time, I'm not sure that's a good idea." Mike looked at me, left eyebrow raised. "You know, I could go with you," he offered.

"Thanks, but no," I told him. "I need you to stay here, get ready for winter, and finish up the blueprints we discussed while I am gone. We will have refugees soon."

"How do you figure?" Now his right eyebrow was up; he was bewildered. "We haven't seen anyone for months!"

"True," I agreed. "But God told me many more people are coming." I was confident.

"So you want me to stay here just in case some people show up while you're gone? Again, Lilly, we didn't see anyone on our way from Bad Axe, and you have been alone for two years."

"Not entirely alone. We ran into the Fates' army, the Furies, about five months ago near town." I paused for a moment before adding, "and it's not *if*, but *when*. You will know them by their knowledge of our Lord Jesus Christ. Ask them what verse they have read today, and they will reply with 'Zephaniah 3:17.' That," I instructed, "is how you will know they are safe to let in."

"Okay, so you just gave a good reason why you shouldn't go alone," Mike replied in disbelief.

"You know, Mike, I just can't understand why you still don't believe God speaks to me."

He shrugged.

"Why don't you ask God yourself then?" I said, slightly irritated, thinking, *What more proof does he need?* I was not the same person I had been when we first met at church fifteen years ago.

They will come. Mike will see. Trust Me.

I trust You, Lord.

Sarah called up to us: "Dinner is ready. Come on down before it's all gone."

I picked up my backpack, glared at Mike, and silently walked past him. There was nothing more to say just then. *God will protect me.* I strolled slowly down the stairs. I hadn't put my black steel-toed combat boots on, and the wooden stairs made for a slippery step.

"I see you've changed and packed," Sarah said while glaring at Mike, who was just behind me. She was signaling her disdain with the outcome to him.

Mike shrugged and sat down quietly at the table. Much to my surprise, all five kids were seated and had their plates and mugs ready. The dogs were not inside.

"You look like a boy!" Clair blurted. "Why are you dressed like that?"

"Like *what*, honey?" I asked.

She laughed. "You have on a green army jacket, cargo pants, big black boots, and a hat to hide your hair!"

"You're very observant," I said with a wink. "I'm not trying to make a fashion statement. It's so I can blend into the trees and appear as a man during the day. That way people who are wandering won't bother me."

"You're so smart, Miss Lilly," Clair said. She smiled and said nothing more.

Sarah sighed. "So I see you still intend to leave?"

"Yes, I am leaving at sundown," I replied tersely, and I then spoke slowly. "The alternative is not good. I don't have a thyroid. Period. I must find a pharmacy or somehow get more medication that keeps me going."

"I understand that," Sarah said. "I'm just questioning your decision to go alone … after what happened in Bad Axe in the war between Canada, the Michigan militia, and the Furies."

"Yes, it was brutal," I admitted.

"Exactly," Sarah said. "The Furies bombed the Blue Water Bridge, burned down the surrounding land, and took all survivors captive, driving us out of our home!"

"I know," I said, recalling the tragedy that occurred two years ago. "Remember, though, Canada is defending the Michigan side of the Blue Water Bridge. The Michigan militia pushed the Furies back toward Detroit, as you told me yesterday. We haven't seen any of them in a few weeks. That's why I need to go *now*, before the Furies decide to come back and destroy more of mid-Michigan."

"Point," Sarah conceded.

"Just trust in God," I said. "Cast your cares on Him. He said the timing was right. Besides, trust me on this: you don't want to witness what happens when I have no hormones. I'll go insane and eventually die. Pray for me, and let's hope I'll be back soon, preferably before the ground frosts over."

"Then it's settled," Sarah said, standing behind Mike with her hand atop his shoulder. "I'll make sure the kids are taken care of as we prepare for winter."

I looked across the table at them. Sarah and Mike acted so much alike that they could almost be mistaken for siblings. I had known them for over fifteen years now. We met when the children were small.

Mike stood five feet six with a stocky frame, green eyes, red hair, and a long reddish-brown beard. Sarah was slightly shorter with a thin frame, brown eyes, and long, straight platinum-blonde hair. I sat at one end of the table directly across from John, with the little ones in between. The kids had all been thin before the world changed; now they were frail. The sun had begun to set and was casting shadows on their pale, thin faces.

"Let's pray," Mike began." Lord Jesus, thank You for protecting our families and providing food during these challenging times. Bless the food to our bodies. Protect Lilly and direct her steps as she journeys to find the life-saving medication. Thank You for everything You do for us. In Jesus's name, amen."

"Amen," we all echoed.

"Let's eat!" Jeremy and Kyle shouted.

"What do we have to eat, Mom?" Elise asked.

Sarah carried the large wooden bowl over to the table and began serving the children.

"Salad again," Clair whined.

"It's salad or nothing," Sarah replied.

"Be grateful we have any food at all," Mike scolded. "Remember last winter?"

Clair nodded and began eating, humbled because during the previous winter they practically starved before walking to my farm. Whether from reflection or hunger, we all ate in silence. Although they were sixteen and seven, respectively, Elise and Clair had experienced far more than they should have in their short lives. The same was true for their brothers Jeremy and Kyle, both of whom were tall and rail-thin. They took care of each other, and most of the time, they all got along. They were still kids, though, and I could forgive a kid almost anything.

The utter silence around the dinner table seemed to last forever before I broke it. "This salad is delicious." It consisted of tomatoes, cucumbers, peppers, black beans, fresh dill, and parsley. Sadly, we had run out of dressing a year and a half ago, along with cheese and chocolate and bacon bits.

"Hmm," I sighed.

"What are you sighing about, Mom?" John asked between bites of a luscious red tomato.

"Of all the things I miss," I said, "chocolate-covered bacon is near the top." I laughed.

We all laughed.

"Well, at least you are alive," John said. "*If* life is even worth living without chocolate-covered bacon."

I laughed again.

"Me? I miss cheddar cheese," John said.

"I miss strawberry ice cream," Jeremy chimed in.

"It's sour candy for me," Kyle said.

"I miss pickle-flavored chips," Clair said.

"Me too, and french onion dip!" Elise added.

"Pizza and wings," Mike and Sarah said at once.

"Buffalo, teriyaki, barbecue," Mike said.

"And lemon pepper," Sarah said, shaking her head.

"This isn't helping," John said, smiling.

"For all we don't have," I said, "we have an awful lot to be thankful for."

"Amen," Mike said.

"And we have something else to be thankful for right now," Sarah announced, rising from the table and fetching a large bowl from the counter. "Voilà! We have fruit for dessert. Tonight we have blueberries, blackberries, and strawberries picked fresh today." Sarah passed the fruit bowl to me.

"I thought of something else I miss," I said. "Whipped cream."

"Mmm, yum," the kids echoed. "Whipped cream."

If only we had some cows, we could make whipped cream, fresh butter, ice cream. We didn't have sugar, but we did have sugar beets. A cocoa tree would be lovely too. The last time John and I ventured out, I noticed that the cows, pigs, and chickens from the surrounding farms were either dead or missing. We did manage to find some corn and grains, though. That first winter, we made a loaf of unleavened bread when the indoor garden didn't grow as fast as anticipated and the fish failed to multiply.

Six-plus more mouths to feed this winter was going to be a struggle without preparation. The good news was that I noticed a herd of deer roaming nearby yesterday. I hoped the wild turkeys were returning as well. I hadn't seen deer or turkeys since the world changed. I made a mental note to send the boys out on a hunting expedition when I returned. The girls would have to harvest and can the outdoor apples, pears, and plums. I stared out the window at the fruit trees in the distance. I expected the plum trees to produce fruit this year, as the immature fruit was already showing.

"What are you looking at, Mom?" John asked.

"Nothing, really, just thinking about all the work to be done before winter. While I'm gone, you boys spend some time making more arrows and traps, and do some target practice. When I return, you will all need to go on a hunt for deer, rabbits, turkeys, and maybe a squirrel or two."

"Cool!" Kyle said. "Now we're getting to the good part."

"Guess we should get started," John said. "Can we be excused? We can go make some arrows and target practice out back."

"Sure," I said. "Give me a hug first. I will be leaving soon. I love you."

John gave me a big hug and didn't seem to want to let me go. "Be careful, Mom, and I'll see you when you get back."

"You will," I said.

"I love you, Mom."

At the door, he looked back and gave me a wink.

"What can we girls do to help prepare for winter?" Elise asked.

"You two need to learn how to can the fruits from the outside trees and vines. I see that you and John didn't have time to can the berries today. There is a blue binder in the kitchen cabinet by the fridge titled 'Canning Instructions.' Read it over and ask John if you need help. You will have to can them before the week's end."

"Okay," Elise said. "Come on, Clair; let's get the binder and go upstairs and read this binder before nighttime."

Elise got the binder, and the two girls trotted upstairs.

*　　*　　*

I went downstairs. I had the scant provisions locked in a basement room to ration. The cellar had old, scratchy beige carpeting. Against the far wall was an old black leather sofa and a small child-sized cot. A bookcase with various literary works and shelves lined with pictures of times past was to the left of the stairs, framing the wooden desk. To the right of the stairs was the rations room, behind a standard white door. It could easily be mistaken for a closet.

I unlocked the rations room door and realized I would need to leave someone in charge of the rations. But who? I was considering Mike. He is a logical man, practical, and wouldn't go on an eating binge. We had been friends for many years now, and though we had our differences, I could still trust him.

Separating power would be a good thing. At eighteen, John was a bit young to make all the decisions, and the burden would weigh heavily on his compassionate soul. The small rations room housed a fridge, five standing freezers, and ten rows of almost empty metal shelves, which were made for a garage. When the fish failed to multiply during year one and the garden ceased to grow, we ate mainly from the dehydrated foodstuffs, the rations.

"Hmm, what to take with me?" I spoke aloud to an empty room, as I often did. I gathered the last of the water bottles—five twenty-ounce bottles, to be exact. I could always refill them using the metal filter bottle. I collected a few pouches of dehydrated food, protein bars, and a collapsible dog bowl for Ice's water. I estimated that the food should sustain Ice and me for about a week. We had survived on less in the past. As I turned to close the door to the rations room, I spotted the last two jars of homemade pickles near the back shelf.

"I think I could fit those in the middle of the backpack as long as they are not next to my thyroid medicine or the dehydrated food." I got the bottles. I closed the door to the rations room, locked it, and then walked to the bookcase against the opposite wall.

I moved the bookcase, exposing the wall safe behind it, which held gold, silver, silver coins, guns, and ammunition. I grabbed the last two slim gold bars and a few silver bars and hid them in the folds of the blanket in my backpack. After returning the shelf to normal, I went back up to the kitchen. The whole house was still. Mike and Sarah had cleaned the kitchen and were sitting on the sofa in the living room, talking in hushed voices.

"Am I interrupting something?" I asked.

"No," Mike answered. "We were just marveling at the incredible detail in your winter prep guide."

"There's a lot in there," I said. "Do you have any questions about the winter prep guidelines?"

"No, it's straightforward," Sarah said. "We haven't done anything like this before, though."

"Well, you have John. He will be a lot of help. He did everything in the guide along with me. There are grids for the amount of food we need to can before winter hits, depending on the number of people. Count on having at least six more people."

"Will do," Mike said.

"I need you two to take charge of the ration room," I said, handing Mike the key.

He immediately put the chain holding the key around his neck, hiding it from sight under his shirt.

"Okay," Mike said. "But how will we know when to use the rations versus eating the fresh produce? Should we follow the current schedule?"

"No, eat all fresh foods every day now; the fall harvest will be plentiful. The rations are low and consist mostly of baby food and formula. The boys will need to hunt when I get back, and the rest of you will need to can any fruit and vegetables left over from the outdoor fall harvest. Keep the compost going, and plow over the fields if I'm gone that long. Save the tops of all root vegetables and soak them in the bin in the greenhouse. They will need to be planted inside for a second winter harvest. Also, there is a food schedule in the back of the binder titled 'Dangerously Low Rations Schedule.' Follow that protocol as needed."

"Of course," Sarah said. "With all these guides, I think we will be able to handle it."

"Maybe we should eat the baby food," Mike joked.

"The puréed prunes are the best," I said, rolling my eyes. "But seriously, the babies will be here soon."

Mike cocked his head. "How do you figure?"

I looked him square in the eye and said, "God said the twins would arrive soon and to prepare for their coming."

"Okay, then," he said. "If you are sure you heard from God. We didn't see anyone on our way here—"

"God can see farther than you," I said.

"And I didn't hear God say more people would come."

"Just because God didn't tell *you* doesn't mean God didn't tell me. Ask God to confirm it for you, Mike," I said, trying not to let agitation get the best of me.

"Maybe I will," he said.

After a brief pause, I began again. "I know both of you can handle things around here together. Remember: don't let anyone in unless—"

"Unless they respond with 'Zephaniah 3:17,'" Sarah interrupted. "We got it the first ninety-four times you told us." She smiled.

"Should I say it a ninety-fifth time?" I asked. "Seriously, you must remember. It could be life or death."

"Got it," Mike said.

"Mike, for Sunday Bible study, John and I have been reading *Forward* by Dr. David Jeremiah. Pick up on page one seventeen. Any young children under twelve will need weekly schooling in reading, comprehension, and math. Use the children's Bibles downstairs."

"Will do," Mike replied.

"Say," Sarah said, "just how many letters did you send out anyway?"

"I sent out twenty to my friends and family members—the ones who survived the shots anyway," I added with a tinge of sadness.

Sarah stepped in and hugged me, making me feel uncomfortable, as I am not too fond of hugs—except from John and the dogs. I slipped from her embrace and continued. "Most of my family died five years after the XYZ676767-9 booster shot."

"Do you think that's what killed them?" Sarah asked as she sat back down next to Mike.

"Yes, I do. My youngest brother, Ken, and his daughter Maya are the only ones who survived. They moved to Crystal Lake near the Upper Peninsula a few years after Jenny, his wife, dropped dead suddenly. I hope *they* are okay."

"Most of our family died, except for Sarah's youngest sister, Emma. We have not been able to contact her either. We will pray for them and the safety of everyone," Mike replied as he got up and handed me a flashlight, some night-vision goggles, and a metal compass. "For safe travels when the woods are dark," he said.

"Thank you." I put the flashlight in my jeans pocket and hung the glasses from my neck, as the moon was full tonight. I got up and went to the sliding glass door next to the kitchen table.

I walked outside, with Sarah and Mike following. "Boys, come inside to say good-bye!" I shouted.

The kids hurried out and said their sweet and sincere farewells.

John came up last, ambling. I could tell something was wrong. "Why don't you see me out to the gate," I told him.

"Sure," he said, avoiding eye contact with me.

I said good-bye to Mike and Sarah, then blew the dog whistle around my neck. Brody, Thing One, and Thing Two immediately came running at me, jumping and barking as if to say 'What adventure are we going to do now, Mom?' Fire and Ice sat down in front of me stoically, staring me down as if to say 'What are we doing next?'

"Be quiet, crazies. Go lie down!" I sternly commanded Brody, Thing One, and Thing Two.

"Ice, come," I ordered. Ice got up and followed me down the driveway toward the gate while Fire sat there looking at Ice and me as if to say 'Good-bye, see you soon.'

John, Ice, and I walked in silence to the gate. John looked me in the eye and said, "Promise me, Mom, that you will return."

"John, you must believe God will look after us and bring us home. He has taken care of us and brought us thus far, right? Continue to pray for me without ceasing. I love you, and you are ready to lead with or without me. You have the walkie. Keep it on and close. I will contact you when I am able. Please don't contact me. You never know who else may be listening." John nodded and hugged me, tears streaming down his handsome face.

"Oh, I made this for you," he said. He reached into his jeans pocket and pulled out what looked to be two thick black leather bracelets. "They are assassin's blades. See, this button goes under your wrist, and you push the circular button, and the blade pops out. Hold out your hands. I'll put them on you."

As John slipped the bracelets on my wrists and tightened the bands, I said, "I hope I don't hurt myself with these." I laughed nervously.

"You won't, Mom." He smiled. "Have faith."

I placed my hands at my sides and stared at John, amazed at the young man who stood before me who had replaced the tiny miracle baby I so cherished. Now that I had lost weight, he could lift me with ease. He towered over me at his height, with lean muscles, a broad chest from spending hours weightlifting, and pale skin that often tanned in the sun. He was clean-shaven and had blue eyes, and brownish hair with blond highlights.

People often said we looked like siblings or a couple, as John's maturity made him seem older and my baby face made me seem younger. I usually wore my long dirty-blond hair in a ponytail, and it accented my blue eyes.

"I love you, Mom." John hugged me again, then released me and knelt beside Ice. "I love you, Ice," he said while hugging him. Ice whined, wiggled out of John's grip, tail wagging, and began to follow me through the gate.

I turned and waved as John closed the gate behind us.

Chapter 2

The Long Road

In all thy ways acknowledge him, and he shall direct thy paths.

—Proverbs 3:6 KJV

Ice and I walked a whole night northwest from the farm, guided by moonglow and starlight, stopping only to rest and eat. We stuck to the woods and backroads to be safe. I didn't want to end up in a burned-out city under the Fates' control a month from now. I hadn't been this way since the world changed.

When John and I left, on day one hundred, we went southeast of the farm to the main town, where we ran into the Furies. We escaped them by trading weapons and an electric car for a second time, to save our lives. There were only a few Furies around back then.

As the sun's rays began to peek through the trees, we came to what appeared to be a major paved road. The DOT signs had been removed and replaced with cardboard signs. The signs read "Fates" and had arrows pointing southeast. *They must not be too bright*, I thought. I knew the cardboard would disintegrate in the first snow or rain shower.

"Well, Ice, it looks like we will continue northwest. I don't want to run into the Fates or their militia, the Furies, ever again."

Ice barked and licked my hand.

I stopped to mark this spot on a map in my journal with a note: "Fates, don't follow."

Ice ran a ways ahead before turning and running back to me, barking and wagging his tail to indicate I should follow him.

"Okay, boy, I'm coming." I followed him slowly, wondering how he had so much energy after walking all night. *Maybe I'm just getting old.*

Ice led me to an abandoned old gas station. The place appeared to have no power, which meant no gas. I followed Ice inside, carefully navigating around the broken glass littering the floor. He kept barking and pawing at the door to a refrigerator made for housing cold drinks. I was not sure why he was doing this, because there were no drinks in the fridge and no food on the shelves. I drew my gun, blew the dog whistle, and motioned downward with my hand to tell Ice to lie down and be quiet. I opened the freezer door very slowly and peered into the darkness.

The horrendous smell that assaulted me caused me to vomit up breakfast. Two dead bodies lay in the back, decaying, covered in what appeared to be fresh blood. I wondered whether the Furies were hiding somewhere, waiting to ambush travelers.

Ice ran to the stack of blankets next to the bodies and began frantically pulling at them, whining, barking, pawing. He was usually not like this. With my left hand cupped over my mouth and nose, I edged closer to the blanket and heard a faint whimpering sound akin to that of a newborn baby. I pushed Ice aside and opened the blanket to find a mixed-breed puppy.

The pure-white female puppy appeared to be about three months old. She was severely malnourished. Just then I noticed the pup's mother lying dead in the laps of its owners. The mother dog appeared to have died from malnutrition and was clinging to her owners, both of whom had bullet holes in their foreheads.

Who could do such a thing?

You know who.

The Fates, of course. I picked up the puppy and closed the refrigerator door, thankful that the smell stayed inside. The puppy immediately began to nuzzle my face, licking and sniffing and trying to get into my backpack, obviously hungry.

"Should we keep her, Ice?" I asked.

Ice barked and wagged his whole body as if to say "Yes we should!" I walked with her around the gas station store, relishing the puppy breath, which I hadn't smelled in many years. The formerly stocked shelves now held only garbage and dust. I made my way to the back of the store, where I saw a locked room bearing a sign marked "Employees Only."

"Hello," I called while knocking.

Silence.

I should look to see if there are any supplies left back here. I pulled the knife out of my backpack and began to pick the rusty padlock. After many attempts, the rusty old lock gave, and I opened the door. The little room had a small metal desk with work schedules and a security camera. It appeared to be the manager's office. I rummaged through the metal desk drawers and found only a lot of business papers. The place had obviously been picked over.

I noticed stairs leading to a loft. "Maybe it's a storage loft," I explained to Ice and the puppy.

I closed the door to the room and barricaded it with the heavy metal desk. Then I set my backpack down and left the puppy with Ice as I climbed the ladder into the loft. The loft was hot, dusty, and a bit creepy. It smelled like rotting food and mold. *Yuck.* Two-year-old defrosted frozen foodstuff. I quickly surveyed the loft and found some nonperishables in the back. I grabbed three thirty-two-ounce red Gatorades, a carton of Slim Jims, two sealed water bottles, a small bag of dog food, and some Biggs pickle-flavored sunflower seeds. Then I climbed down the ladder, closing the loft door behind.

"Look what I found, Ice and puppy—buried treasure! Food."

They both barked and wagged their tails.

I sat on the floor, and both dogs mauled me—especially the puppy, who was barking and clawing at the food in my hands.

"Sit down," I commanded sternly. Ice sat and growled at the puppy until the puppy finally sat down dejectedly next to him.

"Thank You, Jesus, for this delicious food," I prayed.

I opened the dog food and emptied half of it on the ground next to them. The dogs hungrily dug into the mound. I drank half of each water bottle and poured the remainder into the dog bowl from my backpack. I opened the Slim Jim box and ate two, washing them down with a Gatorade.

"We will sleep here today," I said while pulling a blanket from my backpack to use as a pillow. As soon as I lay down, Ice picked up Puppy by the scruff of her little neck and set her on top of me. Then he lay down with his head at my feet, and I fell quickly into the darkness of sleep.

I awoke sometime later as the sun was setting. The dogs were sleeping peacefully, snoring softly with every breath. I filled the metal dog bowl with the last of the water I had brought.

They both awoke immediately and began to drink it. I fed them the rest of the kibble while eating a Slim Jim and drinking Gatorade. Then I took my backpack up to the loft and filled it with the rest of the food as well as a recently discovered can of Cheez Whiz and some mini chocolate bars. I took my meds after eating knowing full well it would lower their efficacy, better late than never, I thought, and surveyed the room one last time. Behind the counter, I found some dog food, aspirin, vitamins, and cold medicine in the corner. I took all that would fit in my backpack.

Ice whined.

"Potty?" I asked.

He answered with a bark. I moved the desk from the office door, and we stepped out into the gas station. Ice took off outside.

"Whoa, girl." I scooped up Puppy and placed her inside my jacket for safekeeping.

I was glad for the full moon. Ice circled back quietly, enjoying the cooling summer night air.

I turned on my walkie and spoke into it. "John, are you there?"

Seconds later, John's voice rang out. "Mom, how are you? Where are you? I miss you!"

"Slow down, and I miss you, too. I'm a day roughly north of our farm. All is we—"

"Did you find medication yet?" he interrupted.

"No, not yet," I replied. "I will walk all night and see where the road leads me."

"Okay," he said. "We are doing fine here and sticking to the binder schedule. I think the kids are starting to feel better. We've been practicing shooting in the backyard. The girls too."

"Great," I said. "Oh, last week on my way out, I saw wild turkeys down by where the deer were grazing last week. The wild animals have finally come back. I am going to turn off the walkie now. Love you, John. Bye."

"Love you, too, Mom," he said. "Bye." I heard a click as he turned off the walkie first.

"Thank You, Lord," I prayed. All seemed to be well back home.

The weather had recently begun to change. I hoped to find a pharmacy soon and get back before summer completely gave in to fall and then winter. I really hoped to be back before winter. The best thing about Michigan is the summer nights, with the cool breeze and moonlit skies making for beautiful evenings as the summer season draws to an end. The world had changed, but that had not. I took out my headphones and turned on the solar-powered device to listen to *Thru the Bible* by Dr. J. Vernon McGee. His sermons made sense to me. I could hear God through him. Dr. McGee had been dead more than fifty years, but his message, God's message, through him lived on. Some day in heaven, I hope to meet Dr. McGee and tell him how much his sermons helped me.

The dogs and I walked under cover of the woods the whole night. Just as the sun was rising, we came upon a tiny vacant cabin hidden in the woods.

"Come on, Ice," I said as I opened the front door. "Maybe we will find a bed."

Ice ran past me and sat down on the dusty rug in the middle of the main room of the small cabin. It had one bedroom and a kitchen made up of 1950s-type metal appliances. The plaster walls were white and dirty, and cobwebs filled the corners. Everything was covered in dust or dirt. The place appeared to be someone's summer cabin. Before the world changed, people would come out to these parts to hunt during the fall and swim in the multiple massive lakes throughout the summer.

I placed Puppy on the ground next to Ice and closed and locked the front door. There was a small wooden table with two chairs in the kitchen and a small bed—a cot, really—in the tiny bedroom. I dragged a chair over from the kitchen table and wedged it against the front door, just in case. The cabin had a single very dirty window and a few white cabinets surrounding the old gas kitchen stove. I looked through the cupboards and found some dry dog food, canned soup—*Chicken noodle, yum*—and some bottled water. I was thankful there were a lot of dog owners around!

"Dinner time!" I called to the dogs as I dumped the dried dog food on the ground, too tired to search for a bowl.

The dogs inhaled the food and water, and I inhaled some Slim Jims and then moved to the bedroom. Ice jumped up onto the bed while the puppy sat whimpering, as her legs were too short to jump up onto the bed.

"Here you go, little one," I said, picking her up by the scruff of her neck and plopping her onto the mattress.

I yawned and decided to call John on the walkie before going to bed. "John, are you there?" No reply. "John!"

"Hi, Mom!" John said, his voice gravelly. "I just woke up. It's early."

"I know." I yawned. "I'm about to lie down to sleep, but I wanted to say hi first. I miss you."

"I miss you, too, Mom. I'm all right. Not much is going on here. Same as yesterday. Where are you now?"

"In a small cabin in the woods. All is well. Okay, I love you. I need to go to sleep now. I'm tired too."

"Love you, too. Bye, Mom!" John exclaimed as he signed off.

I lay down on the bed with Ice beside me and Puppy lying next to my head on the pillow. I noticed that the pillow felt extremely hard. I placed Puppy on top of Ice, sat up, and reached into the pillowcase and pulled out a red hardcover journal. The pages were yellowing as if they had been there many years. I opened the journal and, to my surprise, found the first few pages blank. Somewhere near the middle, there was one page with writing on it.

To my dearest love, Agnus!

I have waited as long as I dare for you to return. The Fates are coming for me. I am sorry I got you caught up in this mess. I pray you are safe. I must leave now to avoid capture. I will meet you at our hiding place. Stay safe.

Love always,
Saul

That was it. The rest of the pages were blank. I lay back down and wondered who these people were, what they were involved in, and whether they made it back to each other as I fell asleep.

*   *   *

Some hours later, I awoke to the sound of the puppy crying in the darkness. I rose slowly from the bed, went into the kitchen, and let the dogs out. A quick scan of the bathroom cupboard and bedroom drawers turned up no medicine. *Time to keep moving,* I thought as I picked up my bag and went out.

"This way!" I called to the dogs, and I set out walking in the same direction as yesterday, hoping to find a pharmacy soon.

Have faith.

Please, God, help me have faith.

A few miles later, we came upon what looked to be a burned-out small town. *It must have been the Furies,* I thought. *But why? What were the Fates looking for in Michigan?*

You know what—the twins. The Fates want the twins.

Why?

Silence.

"Come on, pups, follow me!" I commanded, motioning for the dogs to follow me around the burned-out houses they wanted to enter.

"Ugh, nothing salvageable here!"

Ice stopped and let out a "Urrrrh?" He looked at me and turned his head from side to side.

"I know, you're a good boy!" I said, stroking his fur. "It's not your fault!"

Ice wagged his tail and ran off ahead of me and joined Puppy. Ice seemed to understand what I wanted. I kept walking until I neared the last of the burned-out houses. The dirt road had turned into gravel and ended abruptly at the edge of some woods. *That's odd,* I thought, expecting there to be a building or home. All I saw were overgrown bushes, tall grass, and trees.

"Ice, where are you?!" I called, and then I whistled.

Seconds later, Ice emerged from some low-hanging branches. He stood there looking at me, jerking his head back several times, beckoning me to follow him. Then he turned and began to run back into the brush. I followed him slowly down the gravel road and through the trees, twigs snapping under my feet. I came out of the thick brush and woods in front of a white building. In the moonlight, I had difficulty determining what type of vacant building it was. It appeared to be neither burned-out nor inhabited.

I scaled the front steps leading onto the porch and read the sign on the front door: "Little Angels Veterinarian Clinic." I pushed open the heavy oak door.

"Ruff!" Ice and Puppy barked somewhere in the darkness.

I switched on the flashlight and found a virtually new country vet clinic. Looking around, I found a little waiting area with a wooden bench, a few chairs, and a small table with some brochures and patient information sheets on it. Just beyond the waiting area was a check-in counter, behind which was a small desk, an office chair, and a few filing cabinets. To the right was a patient room with an exam table. On the back wall behind the desk was a door leading to a back room, where Ice and Puppy appeared. I wedged the wooden table against the front door and went into the back room.

"Another vacant building," I sighed.

No, he's coming. He's late.

Who?

Trust me.

"Ruff, ruff, ruff!" Ice interrupted, wagging his tail excitedly.

"Oh no," I said. "Did you find another puppy?"

"Urh?" he tilted his head and then pointed his nose toward a cage in the back right corner of the room.

"Ice, I need to find medicine!" I exclaimed. "All right, I'm coming."

I walked toward the back wall. As I approached Ice, I shone the flashlight on an operating table, a lot of surgical supplies, and a few cages to hold the tiny patients. Though I could hear no animals, Ice would not stop whining as I rummaged through the cabinets.

"Be quiet!" I commanded. "There aren't any animals in here!"

Ice sat down, softly whining, and stared intently at the dark rear left corner of the room. Puppy sat with him. "Just be patient," I told the dogs. "I've found some more buried treasure." I packed up the first-aid supplies, some heartworm pills, rabies vaccinations, and new syringes.

I opened a bag of dog food I found in the cupboard and emptied half of it on the floor. "Eat," I said. The surgical sink was still working, so I filled a metal bowl with water. "Drink."

Ice didn't budge. "Grrrr," he growled, low and deep, still staring into the dark corner.

"When *you* refuse food, it's serious," I said. "All right, I'm coming."

I stroked Ice's head gently, and he fell silent but sat perfectly still and stared intently into the darkness. In the glow of the flashlight I saw a table holding a small cage for hamsters, gerbils, guinea pigs, or rats. It was so dark that even with the flashlight I couldn't see very well. I could smell, however, and the odor of feces as I approached told me something was alive in there.

"Hey there, little one," I said, gently placing the folded back of my finger against the cage bars. An average-sized male albino rat approached me hesitantly. He sniffed my finger, whiskers twitching cutely, then hurried to the back of the cage.

"How are you still alive?" Someone had to be taking care of him. Maybe the person had been captured or had left in search of food. I could only hope he or she was friendly. I scanned the flashlight over and around the cage and saw that both the water and food bowls were almost empty.

I picked up the patient chart and read. "Pinky is a one-year-old male rat in for neutering. The procedure went well. This brilliant boy is something of an escape artist and knows many tricks. He is somewhat friendly."

Ice approached the cage and stood face-to-face with Pinky as they sniffed each other through the bars.

"You want to keep him?" I asked.

"Urff!" Ice replied, wagging his tail.

"Well, I'm not carrying this cage around!"

"Urrh?" Ice pointed to a slightly open drawer to my left.

"What?" I held up my hands in exasperation.

Ice opened the drawer with his teeth and pulled out what looked like a metal harness for Pinky. He brought it over and dropped it at my feet. He kept looking from me to Pinky and back to me.

"Ruff!" He began to wiggle his whole body with urgency.

"Okay, okay," I said. "I get it. Just calm down." I picked up the harness and then opened Pinky's cage.

"It's okay, Pinky." I extended my hand toward him, palm up. "You're the escape artist, but we're going to break you out. Come on, let's go."

Pinky sniffed my fingers, then darted toward the open door. I grabbed him before he could escape, slid the blue metal harness onto him, and placed him in my pocket. Pinky quickly settled down and fell asleep. I went back out front and sat down on the office chair behind the counter. Some time later, I heard the rattling of a lock coming from the back of the clinic.

"Hush!" I blew the whistle for Ice to lie down beside me as I dropped to the floor and drew my gun. I couldn't see very well, but I could hear what sounded like metal being dragged across the floor and heavy footsteps.

"Pinky!" a familiar-sounding male voice shouted. "Where are you?!"

Ice bolted, ignoring my commands, and leaped up and knocked whoever it was to the ground and stood there licking his face.

Laughing, the man pushed him off as I sneaked up on him.

"Stop! Don't move!" I commanded. I shoved the muzzle of my gun against the base of his skull while Ice finally sat beside me.

The man raised his hands while standing up and turning to face me. "I mean you no harm."

"Who are you?" I said, easing back toward the office, where it was easier to see by moonlight. "And why are you here?"

"Relax," he said, hands still up. "My name is Jaden. I won't hurt you."

"You got that right," I said. I was the one with the gun trained on *him*.

"I used to work here. But what I really want to know is how you got Pinky out of the cage. He bites me." Jaden took a step toward me.

"Stop right there," I commanded. "Don't come any closer." I directed him to step into the ray of light streaming through the nearby window so I could see the young man better. His voice sounded so familiar; I just couldn't place it.

"Lilly, is that you? I haven't seen you in over twenty years, since high school graduation."

"Oh," I replied, and I lowered my gun.

"Do you remember? We attended St. Bartholomew's High School together. We met at the homecoming football game first year and hung out a lot."

"We did," I said. "Now I remember." I sat back down on the metal chair. "Are you chipped? Show me your arm!"

"Was," he said, stretching out his arm. "Look, I dug it out when the world changed." He pointed to a three-inch scar, jagged—obviously a homemade effort.

"You?" he asked.

"I never got chipped." I showed him both my forearms.

"Wow, I like your tattoos!" he said, reading: "Zephaniah 3:17: 'The LORD thy God in the midst of thee is mighty; he will save, he will rejoice over thee with joy; he will rest in his love, he will joy over thee with singing.' And Isaiah 55:8 KJV: 'For my thoughts are not your thoughts, neither are your ways my ways, saith the LORD.'"

"Two of my favorites," I said, rolling down my sleeves.

He nodded. "It's been so long. Why are *you* here, and who are your friends?" Jaden bent down and picked up Puppy, cuddling him in his long, gangly arms. Jaden had always been tall and thin with light brown skin, green eyes, and a clean-shaven head; none of that had changed.

"I could ask you the same thing," I said.

"You already did," he reminded me.

"Well, you shouldn't sneak up on a woman like that. I almost shot you."

"So that thing's loaded, eh?" he said, smiling. "Fair enough. I'll go first. I worked here as a vet tech before the power grid went down. A few weeks ago, my wife and I were searching for food. We planned to meet up here if we ever got separated. So here I am waiting for Susan to arrive."

I hesitated before responding. Jaden seemed sincere. "Me, I'm looking for medicine. The big dog's name is Ice. I've had him for years. The small puppy we found at a gas station a few days ago. She doesn't have a name. I call her Puppy."

"Original," he said playfully. "So what kind of medicine do you need? We have antibiotics here."

I rolled my eyes and laughed. "You did. I took all the vials of animal medicine I could find, and unfortunately you don't have what I need— thyroid meds."

"There is a small town just southwest of here. The town might still have medicine in the pharmacy." Jaden picked up Puppy and inspected her. He opened one of the drawers I had not gotten around to rummaging through and pulled out a syringe filled with yellow liquid. He squirted it into Puppy's mouth. "This puppy has worms. Take these and give her one a day for a week, and give Ice one as well." He set Puppy down on the floor and gave Ice a larger syringe of liquid.

"Thank you," I said, putting the syringes in my bag. "We must be going now." I turned to leave.

"So soon? Don't you trust me?"

I glared at him. He was oblivious and must have forgotten what he had done to me all those years ago, how he had turned against me and stood by while the entire football team bullied me mercilessly.

I don't trust him, and people don't change.

You can trust him. My world has changed him.

"You may not remember."

He squinted and shrugged.

"You hurt me in high school when you didn't stand up for me in front of your friends. I had no one, and I felt lost." I was surprised that I began crying as the years of torment bubbled to the surface of my memory again. I let the gun drop to my side.

"I was a dumb kid," he said, shaking his head. "I'm so sorry. I wanted to fit in. I didn't like the bullying either. I have grown up a lot in the last twenty-plus years. I'm really sorry," he said with sincerity.

"I accept your apology, and I forgave you many years ago. I agree. We were dumb kids. I do need to sleep," I said, yawning, "and the sun is almost up."

"You travel at night then?"

"Yes, it's safer. If possible, I stick to dirt roads and woods."

"That's wise," he said. "Come back here to the break room." He motioned for me to follow him to a room behind the operating room that I had not noticed.

The room had a table, chairs, a small fridge, a bank of white cabinets, and a sink.

"This is perfect!" I said as I quickly wedged a chair under the door handle.

"Why did you lock us in?" he asked.

"I just don't want any surprises. It's not safe out here." I paused before saying, "You haven't run into the Fates yet?"

"No, we hid in our farmhouse, north of here, until a few days ago. I have heard of the Fates from other travelers, though; best to stay away from them. People say they are evil."

"Did you happen to learn where the Fates' camp is?"

"Actually, yes," Jaden replied. He was riffling through the cupboards, apparently searching for food. "Awesome!" He turned to me, smiling.

"Gold mine—instant coffee, chips, and water! Here." He tossed me a bag of plain Better Made chips and a bottle of spring water. "Let's save the coffee for tonight!"

"Good idea." I opened the chips and water.

Jaden finished his small bag of chips in a few bites and then sat down on the ground. "To answer your question, I heard the Fates' camp is somewhere in the mountains of eastern Tennessee."

"That's odd. So then why are the Fates here?" I wondered out loud, to see if Jaden knew.

"I don't know. The militia thinks the Fates are looking for someone or something."

The twins. You must find them soon, Lilly.

"Well, let's hope the Fates don't find who they are looking for and leave soon! I'd rather not run into them again!"

"It would be nice not to have to hide anymore." Jaden paused. "You look exhausted. I can keep watch if you want to sleep? I stick to a normal schedule—sleep at night." He smiled.

"All right, just for a few hours." I lay down on the cold cement floor with the dogs curled up at my feet and Pinky asleep in my pocket.

"Mom!" John shouted. "Mom, are you there?"

I grabbed the walkie from my backpack. *Uh-oh, must be an emergency, for I told John not to call me.* "I'm here, John. What is it?"

"I'm sorry I called, but Kyle got sliced with a knife, and Mr. Tim doesn't have a needle and thread to sew up the wound. Do we have one?"

An unfamiliar deep male voice spoke in the background: "Hurry, Kyle's losing a lot of blood."

"In my closet, on the top shelf, there is a purple-and-yellow sewing kit," I told him. "There is a pint of vodka behind it to sanitize everything with. Give a shot or two of vodka to Kyle to dull the pain."

"Hold on, Mom," John said, pausing. I could hear only muffled voices at this point. "Great, thanks, Mom. Mr. Tim found the needle and thread. He will be able to sew Kyle up. I need to go help now. Love you. Bye." John clicked off the walkie before I had a chance to respond.

"Everything okay?" Jaden asked.

"Yes, that was my son John. The others will help him."

"Get some sleep. Good night, old friend."

"Good night," I replied, closing my eyes and falling quickly into a deep slumber.

*   *   *

The thick snowflakes fell rapidly in the vast field where I stood shivering. *Where is my coat?* I thought as I began jumping up and down to keep warm. The snow soaked through the thin red slippers on my feet and started to freeze. I saw the light in the distance and began running toward it.

A woman's voice drifted to me, seemingly from the opposite direction. "Lilly, help! Hurry, I need you!" I kept running, blood now pouring down my face. Struggling to breathe, I yelled, "I'm coming; hold on!"

"Hurry! They're coming!"

*   *   *

I awoke disoriented, gasping as I struggled to breathe.

"Lilly, what happened?" Jaden asked, bracing my back to sit me up.

"I had a vision," I said. "I've stayed here too long. I need to go."

"All right," he said. "I made you some dinner. At least have a cup of coffee and some chips with me."

I breathed in the familiar scent of freshly brewed coffee wafting from two cups on the table. "How can I turn down coffee? I guess it would be okay to stay a few minutes longer." I sat down at the table with him.

"Where are the dogs, and what happened to your finger?"

"Pinky bit me when I put him in the hamster ball. I don't understand why he likes you and not me. I'll be all right. The dogs are outside. I just got done feeding them."

"Sorry about Pinky. Most animals like me for some reason." I took a sip of the warm black gold. "Yum, this coffee is so good!"

"Agreed," he said. "I haven't had any coffee since the beginning!"

"What did you do all day while I slept?"

"First I searched the rest of the clinic for supplies but didn't find anything else. Then I read the Bible and prayed for my wife to return," Jaden replied sadly.

"I know she will be back soon. Where will you go?"

"She has family in Texas. Last week, I heard from the militia that Texas is free, and the Fates tried but failed to take over the state. We will head there on foot."

"Sounds like a good plan. If you change your mind, pray, and God will lead you to my house. You are always welcome."

"Thank you," Jaden said. "I will discuss it with my wife, and we will pray about it."

I stood up and whistled for the dogs to return. Ice promptly busted through the door with Puppy at his heels. *Awesome*, I thought. *Ice is training Puppy for me.*

"How did you train the dogs?" Jaden asked. "That's amazing!"

"Before the world changed, I took them to a K-9 training program. I have another dog at home trained this way as well." I took Pinky out of the hamster ball, harnessed him, and set him on my shoulder.

"You should take the ball, too," Jaden suggested as he placed the ball in my backpack.

"Thanks," I said, hugging Jaden. "We really must go now. God bless."

"Bye, Lilly." Jaden waved as I left through the back door into the night, heading southwest with the dogs following close at my heels.

The dogs and I walked the way Jaden had suggested for two hours. The moon began to shrink, leaving a colder, darker night sky. I was thankful for the night-vision goggles and put them on. The dogs kept circling back and forth. We walked on like this for several more hours. So many thoughts rushed through my mind as fatigue began to set in. I needed to find a place for us to sleep before the sun rose and I collapsed from exhaustion. Hours later, as the sun shone high in the sky, we came to another small hunting cabin in the woods.

This was a real log cabin, and the logs appeared to be rotting from age. The door opened to a single room containing a kitchen, bar stool, cot, and bathroom in the back. The dust-covered floor and cot made it appear to be vacant.

"Come on, guys; let's rest!" I commanded the dogs as I shut the door and wedged the stool beneath the doorknob.

No more surprises, I thought while rummaging through the cabinets. To my delight, I found some freeze-dried coffee, canned beef, chicken broth, and cat food. "Here you go, guys, eat!" I commanded while dumping all the cat food on the floor and filling a ceramic bowl with well water from the sink.

"Ow! Stop, Pinky!" I yelled as he had crawled onto my arm and began to nibble on my hand with his sharp little teeth.

"Sit here," I commanded while tying his harness to the spring of the cot in reach of the cat food and water. Pinky joined the dogs in inhaling the cat food and lapping up the water.

I leaned against the counter and took out the walkie. "John, are you there?"

"Hi, Mom," he said groggily. "I'm here. It's early."

"How is Kyle?"

"He's resting. That vodka knocked him out. Mr. Tim got him all sewn up. He said Kyle should be okay."

"Who is Mr. Tim?" I asked.

"He's a nice man," John said. "He was a veterinarian before the world changed. He showed up two nights ago with his daughter Ruby. She doesn't talk, though."

"Okay, well, I will let you go back to sleep. I love you, John."

"Love you too, Mom, bye."

"Ugh, so much dust." I sneezed while shaking out the pillow and blanket before lying down on the cot. "God, forgive me for my sins known and unknown. Help me to know what You want me to do. Protect those fleeing from the Fates. Reunite Saul with Agnus and Jaden with Susan. Keep everyone at home safe. In Jesus's name, I pray. Amen."

I closed my eyes. The dogs jumped up on the cot, waking me up, squeezing me toward the wall while Pinky lay down underneath, running back and forth. I decided to put the nocturnal Pinky in the hamster ball so he could get some much-needed exercise. The sound of Pinky scurrying across the wooden floor, occasionally bumping into a wall, lulled me into a deep sleep.

* * *

"Ruff!" Ice barked while covering my face in sloppy wet kisses.

"All right, I'm up. I'll let you out." I rose and opened the door. Ice and Puppy ran out into the cool early morning.

"Not you, Pinky!" I managed to scoop up the ball before Pinky made it outside.

"Come on, little one; let's eat some breakfast." I pulled him out of the ball, harnessed him, and set him on the kitchen counter.

Ice heard the word "breakfast" and came running back in, pushing the wooden door open on his own. He sat looking intently at me, tail wagging, with the puppy at his side.

"You want breakfast?" I teased.

"Ruff, ruff, ruff!" Ice responded, his body wiggling in excitement as he tried to remain sitting.

"Okay, here you go!" I said, dumping all but a handful of the cat food on the floor and refilling the water bottle.

"Here, Pinky." I opened my hand, placing the rest of the cat food on the counter next to him along with a little dish of water I had found.

I filled up my filtered water bottle from the sink and added the entire package of instant coffee to it. In silence, I ate the beef and drank the chicken broth. When all the food and half a cup of coffee were gone, I decided it was time to leave. The wind whistled outside against only the sound of crickets chirping as I closed the wooden door behind us, setting off in the same direction, still searching for a pharmacy.

Hours passed as I walked on listening to Dr. J. Vernon McGee's *Thru the Bible* all the way. The air smelled clean, so unlike the air in the major Michigan metropolitan areas. The dogs ran energetically, circling me as usual, while Pinky sat cleaning himself in my pocket. Just enough moonlight peeked through the trees to guide my steps.

Some hours later, I came upon a stored called Little Mysteries out in the middle of nowhere. I carefully stepped through the broken glass door. I could see secondhand clothes and various trinkets commonly found in antique shops or thrift stores. The dogs followed me, sniffing the ground intently. The store appeared to be vacant, and garbage and dust littered the floor.

"Urrh, ruff." Ice bolted toward a door leading to the back of the store and began scratching intently, trying in vain to open the door.

"Hush!" I commanded, blowing my whistle. I picked up Puppy before she could make any noise.

"Hello," I called, drawing my gun. "Anyone here?"

No answer. I slowly nudged the door open a crack and saw that it led to a staging area for merchandise and a break room for employees. I couldn't see much, but that all-too-familiar horrific stench assaulted me, causing me to vomit. The smell of death. *Not again*, I thought, closing the door behind me and holstering my gun.

"Urh?" Ice sat there looking back and forth between me and the closed door.

"What is it, boy?" I said.

"Ruff!" Ice urged me to investigate the room again.

"Fine, you stay here!" I covered my nose and mouth with my shirt and reopened the door.

The motion sensor lights worked, for better or worse, illuminating a scene even more disturbing than the one at the gas station. Metal shelves were bowing under the weight of large cardboard boxes stuffed with secondhand clothes, toys, small appliances, and trinkets of every kind. To the left there was a small fridge, a microwave, and a wooden table.

The stench grew stronger as I approached the dark corner of the kitchen. *Ghastly* ... To my horror, a man and a woman were slumped over on their knees, facing opposite back corners of the room. Their heads were blown to pieces.

I lost it and began sobbing. My first instinct was to turn and run as fast and hard as I could to get as far away from the horror as possible.

Help me get through this, Lord. Holy Spirit, give me peace.

Calmer, I moved closer and could see that the blood-soaked woman was holding a red book in her hands. I approached and removed it from her grasp. It was a Bible, originally white leather, now stained red.

"This is horrible! Why is this happening, God? Why did I have to be the one to find them?" Tears streamed down my face.

I have spared My good and faithful servants from the events to come.

"Why haven't you spared me?" I asked.

You told Me you wanted to live be one hundred and twenty. I will protect you. Have faith.

"You're right—*of course*," I sighed. "I'm sorry, God."

Go now, and read Michelle's notes.

I shut the door behind me and walked back to the front of the store and pushed an old metal desk up against the front door and a cabinet up against the broken windows. I sat down in the farthest back corner in the middle of the clothing section. Ice sat next to me, licking the tears from my face, and Puppy climbed into my lap.

As I opened the bloodstained Bible, I sensed a strong feeling of importance.

"Wow." I read the inscription on the first page aloud. "Purchased by Michelle Marie Lonely, December 25, 1940. Zephaniah 3:17." From what I could tell from the skin on the dead woman's arms, she looked too young to be in her eighties. *Maybe the dead woman was Michelle's daughter or a friend*, I thought.

The pages unstained by blood were yellow and worn, with no writing. I shook the book vigorously, and a small piece of paper fell out. I very carefully unfolded the sheet of paper and whispered the handwritten words aloud:

> Dearest Lilly,
>
> I had hoped you would arrive before the Fates did. My husband Larry and I have been praying until the end. Go to the back room, to the gray metal shelf in the far left corner. Behind the shelf, you will find a small metal box. You will need the contents for the twins. We pray for your health and safety.
>
> Love,
> Your sister and brother in Christ, Larry and Michelle

Stunned, I pulled matches from my backpack and burned the letter, while Ice continued to lick my face vigorously. I turned to pet his head and said, "Seeing angels again?" while smiling through the tears.

"Urh," Ice responded happily, wiggling his body.

"Stay!" I commanded as I struggled to stand up on my weary legs.

I drew in a deep breath and held it as I returned to the back room and followed the letter's instructions to the shelf. The metal shelf screeched against the cement floor as I pulled it toward me. I found the small metal box and quickly left the room. To my surprise, inside the box were multiple boxes of brown-colored contact lenses and a diamond wedding ring with a gold band.

What am I supposed to do with these?

Keep them hidden. You will see.

"Okay, guys, let's eat," I said as I buried the small box in my bag and took out the last of the dog food and water. After the dogs ate, we fell asleep on top of my backpack on the floor.

*   *   *

"Hoo, hoo!"

I jolted awake to the sound of an owl perched on a tree close to the broken front window of the store. The owl's giant eyes peered hungrily at Pinky through the window.

"Go away!" I yelled, banging on the window in the darkness while stuffing Pinky into my front coat pocket. "Stop escaping, you little escape artist, or you'll be his breakfast!"

My mental fatigue was intense. I needed to find medicine soon.

"Let's go see if we can find some food," I told the dogs.

Holding my breath, I opened the door to the break room, careful not to look again at the dead bodies. I rummaged through the drawers and cabinets and turned up a single box of herbal tea and one honey nut granola bar.

After picking up the food, I walked to the shelving in the back and found a box of donated foodstuff and carried it back to the front of the store.

Ice and Puppy were as excited as I was and tried to tear open the cardboard box. "Stop! Patience!"

They did their best.

"Here, you guys get some Cheerios and—sorry, no milk—water!" I dumped the whole box of Cheerios on the floor and poured some water into a bowl for them.

"Pinky, you stay close!" I commanded while setting him next to the pile of food and carefully tying his harness around my wrist. There was no sign of the hungry owl.

"Thank you, Jesus, for this food," I said while digging into a box of frosted Cheerios and canned milk.

"Ice, Puppy, where are you?" I stood up and brushed crumbs from my pants and threw the rest of the cereal and canned soup into my backpack.

"Guys?" I walked toward the warehouse.

"Ruff!" Ice barked. He was lying on his side, pawing under a metal clothing rack.

"What are you doing, silly boy!"

"Ruff," Ice responded, now sticking his long snout under the rack.

"Eek! Eek!" Pinky protested, scratching the cement floor with his claws as Ice dragged him out from under the shelf.

"Bad Pinky!" I admonished him as I took his lead from Ice and placed him back in my pocket, retying his leash to my wrist. "How did you manage to get away, you little stinker?"

"Ooh!" I exclaimed, stumbling over a box of clothes, my knee hitting something hard and sharp.

"Look, guys, a Polaroid camera! After all we've been through, let's have a little fun."

"Ice, sit," I commanded, and I placed Puppy at his side.

"Here, this black top hat and spectacles are for you, Ice; and for you, Puppy, this Detroit Tigers hat. And Pinky, sit here, on Ice's shoulder," I said, setting the little guy down and tying his harness to Ice's collar. "But don't move a muscle."

I quickly snapped the picture and scooped Pinky up before he had a chance to escape again. *The photo will be nice to share with the kids*, I thought as I finished shaking the picture so it would develop. I placed it in the pocket opposite Pinky. The dogs shook off their clothing and ran to the door, whining.

"All right, let's go," I said as I picked up my backpack and walked out the back door with the dogs at my heels.

We started in the same direction we had come. Some hours later, the road ended at a fence topped with barbed wire in the middle of the dense woods. My flashlight illuminated a sign hanging from the chain links: "Private Property, Keep Out."

I stopped walking and stared intently at the small house in the distance as a dark feeling of dread and despair washed over me.

What should I do, God?

Move on. This place is evil.

I bypassed the house and began walking quickly in the same direction as before, feeling happy and more at ease when the last section of fencing was behind me.

Many hours later, as the sun was rising, I came to a small red house surrounded by fields littered with dead cornstalks. Cautiously, I approached the house, gun drawn. I whistled for Ice to stay by my side. Somebody had broken out the front right window and left the wooden door slightly open. Inside, a round wooden table took up most of the kitchen. Directly behind it was a small bedroom, vacant and covered in dust.

"Okay, guys, it's clear!" I exclaimed.

"Ruff," Ice responded.

Ice and puppy ran into the kitchen, their noses trained like vacuums on the wooden floor, as I barricaded the door with a kitchen chair and put my gun away. I began rummaging through the cherry wood cabinets in search of dinner. No luck. I plopped down on the single chair at the table and pulled some dog food out of my bag and dumped it on the floor.

The dogs wolfed down the food as I filled their bowl with water from my bag. Finally I nibbled on the last package of dry oatmeal I had in the bottom of my backpack, washed it down with water, and took my medication, forgetting again to take it without food.

"Come on, boys! Bedtime!" I walked into the bedroom and lay on the bed. I fell asleep immediately under the warm, soft red comforter.

*   *   *

"Do you think she is alive?" a high-pitched voice whispered.

I thought I was dreaming.

"I don't know," an equally high-pitched voice responded.

"Poke her, Remy!" the first voice said.

"No, Clarice," Remy said, louder. "*You* poke her!"

"Fine!" Clarice said, and she poked me hard with her index finger.

"Ow! Stop it!" I commanded as I shot upright in the bed. I squinted, adjusting my eyes to the darkness, and saw two thin identical twin girls with pale skin, long black hair, and big blue eyes.

"Why are you in our house?" Remy asked.

"I thought it was empty," I said. "How did you get in?"

"We climbed through the window."

"How old are you?"

"We are both eight years old," Remy responded. "But I am the oldest by two minutes."

"You don't look a minute older than—" I let the joke go. "Where are your parents?"

Clarice sighed and said, "Our father was a commander in the military. The Fates killed him because he didn't want to join their army, many days ago." Tears welled in her pretty blue eyes.

"And our mother," Remy added. "She went hunting two weeks ago when we ran out of food. She said to wait here for her."

"Do *you* have any food?" Clarice asked.

"I have a box of Cheerios," I said. "Here, take it." I handed the box to her.

They devoured the Cheerios in silence.

What should I do now? Should I take them with me?

Silence.

Bang!

"Puppies! You're finally back!" Clarice screeched excitedly as she ran to the front door to greet them.

I glanced quizzically at the interaction and saw that Clarice was holding Pinky in her left hand.

"What's wrong?" Remy asked.

"Ice doesn't let strangers touch him," I said, wide-eyed. "And Pinky bites."

"Oh," Remy said, "my sister is an animal whisperer. All animals love her." I detected a hint of jealousy in her voice as Ice began to growl at her.

"Back away slowly, Remy," I commanded, raising my arm and holding it between her and Ice.

"Fine!" Remy yelled, slowly walking toward the bed.

"Ruff!" Ice replied happily, allowing Clarice to do as she pleased with him.

"It's okay," Remy said. "Besides, I don't like animals anyway." She sat down on the bed next to me, sulking.

"It's getting dark," Clarice said. "I wonder if tonight is the night Mom will come home."

"She's probably dead," Remy said, as cold as ice. "And you will be dead soon too! The Fates come for everyone!"

"Don't say that!" I scolded her. "I'm still alive, and God will protect you if you ask for His help. I am positive your mother is still alive."

"Puh!" Remy said, shrugging. "Sure she is." Then she looked away in silence.

"Yeah, I think she's alive, too." Clarice looked at me. "God will protect her."

"Well, girls, I must be moving on now. Would you like to come with me?"

"No," Clarice said, shaking her head. "We'll wait here for Mommy."

"Clarice, I have something for you." I paused and handed her the Bible. "Study this book and hide Jesus's words in your heart."

"Thank you," she said, smiling. "I will." She sat on the bed and began reading the Bible.

"Barricade this door when I leave," I said sternly. "The Fates may still be around."

"Okay," Clarice said. "I'm going to miss you and the animals." She placed Pinky in my pocket, grabbed a chair, and walked me to the door and saw us out.

I set out again in the same direction as yesterday and glanced behind me at the red house. I saw the girls waving from the window. I waved back, thinking, *Odd children.*

They are scared, little girls.

I figured, but Remy …

Time will tell. She will have to choose.

I walked all night without stopping, listening to the crickets chirp while the dogs played, running ahead and then circling back to me. I wanted to put as much distance between me and Remy as possible. Clarice was so sweet, but Remy scared me.

"God, please send Your angels to minister to Remy, Clarice, and their mother. Watch over them and keep them safe. In Jesus's name, I pray. Amen." I walked the rest of the night in silence.

At last the sun began to rise. The dogs were tired as they strolled along panting at my side. We were all hungry and tired, and I dared not say the "h" word, knowing that Ice would go nuts for food. We walked on a few more hours. My stomach hurt, and my legs felt weak and heavy. Finally we came upon a long dirt road that led to a small hunting cabin hidden in the woods.

Ice pointed and perked up his ears as we neared the cabin, turning his head from side to side. Then he took off sprinting toward the cabin with Puppy close behind.

"Wait, stop!" I yelled, to no avail, as I tried to run after him.

A moment later, he stopped and circled back to me, whining, and then sped off toward the cabin door, which he shoved open and let himself in through.

"Help, help ..." a male voice called faintly.

Uh-oh. The smell of rotting flesh greeted me yet again as I walked through the cabin's front door. Choking back vomit, I asked, "What do you need help with, sir?"

"I can't stand up. The Furies were here. They tortured us and broke one of my legs. My wife is dead," the man cried, motioning toward the bathroom where her dead body lay rotting, soaked entirely in blood.

I hurried over and opened the bathroom windows, covered her body with the blood-soaked towels hanging from the shower curtain rod, shut the door, and stuffed more kitchen towels under the bathroom door, hoping that would contain the horrible stench.

Then I hurried over to the frail old man lying on the floor.

"Sit!" I commanded Ice, pointing to the ground next to the man.

"I have an idea," I said. "Wrap one arm around Ice's back, and we will pull you toward the couch."

"Ow!" he cried in anguish as Ice and I slowly dragged him toward the couch.

"Are you able to pull yourself up now?" I asked.

"Yes, I think so," he said, struggling to reply while hoisting himself onto the tattered old blue couch against the wall, using Ice's back as a brace.

"Thank you," the man said. He managed a smile. "By the way, my name is Eli."

"You are welcome. I'm ... El," I said, not sharing my real name, "and this is Ice, Puppy, and Pinky."

"Pleased to meet you all."

"So tell me exactly what happened here."

"Not going to tell me your real name, are you, *eh?* I don't blame you, but I assure you I'm not dangerous." He winked at me, then continued. "A few days ago, Ben, one of the Furies, came looking for my wife and me. He wanted us to join up with their army. I still don't know how he found us. The cabin isn't even ours. We fled here two months ago when God warned us we were in danger." He paused to cough. "Could you get me a glass of water, please?" he asked politely.

The cabin's interior was painted all white, with a small fridge, a black woodburning stove, and a wooden ladder leading to a loft holding one queen-sized metal cot with a thin yellow quilt. I grabbed a white ceramic cup from the dish rack on the counter, filled it with water from the tap, and brought it to the man.

"Finally," he said, gulping down the water. "I thought I'd die waiting for help."

"I still don't understand why the Furies were looking for you. What did they want?"

"I was the head chemist at Dow Chemical, and my wife, Margie ..." His voice broke, and he clenched his eyes shut against the tears. "She was the head engineer there in charge of experimental nuclear weapons. When the Furies took over Dow Chemical, God instructed us to flee Midland and hide in these woods. Ben tracked us because he wanted us to continue making chemical warheads for him. When we refused, he killed my wife and tortured me, breaking my leg and leaving me to die. I stabilized the ankle somewhat with a belt and the wood molding where the wall meets the floor. However, it won't support my weight."

"Show me your forearms," I said.

"Of course," Eli said, holding his frail arm up and showing me the scars surrounded by purplish bruises. "See, I cut the chip out and left it at Dow. And you?"

"I never got the microchips," I said, letting him inspect my forearms. "See, no puncture wound."

"Nice tattoos," Eli said.

"Yeah, everyone says so!" I smiled. "Do you have any food?"

"Yes, there are some canned goods in the cupboards by the sink. I forgot to tell you: Zephaniah 3:17 is my favorite verse."

"My real name is Lilly," I said, smiling. "I will make us dinner." I rummaged through the cupboards for food.

"It's nice to meet you, Lilly." He smiled through his obvious physical and emotional pain.

"Do you want mac and cheese with vienna sausages or black beans?" I asked.

"Let's go with vienna sausages," he replied.

I set about making dinner while Eli rested. I was so happy to have mac and cheese and canned milk again. When dinner was finally ready, I pushed the table over to Eli and moved a chair across from him and sat down.

"Dinner smells delicious. Thank you," he said as I placed large bowls of food and two glasses of milk on the table.

Eli began to pray. "Thank You, God, for bringing me help and for this food. Please bless it to our bodies and keep us safe. Amen. Let's eat!"

"Amen!" I echoed, diving into the bowl and guzzling down the milk.

Ice and Puppy began to whine while Pinky nibbled on my ear.

"Oh, sorry. I forgot you guys are hungry too. I didn't see any dog food, though. Here's some water," I said, and I filled their bowl with water, which they lapped up quickly.

"I've got some venison bones in the fridge," Eli said. "I smoked the bones in the fire, so they should be okay for the dogs to eat."

"Marvelous!" I said. I retrieved the bones and threw them down to the dogs, who immediately began devouring them.

"Here, Pinky." I set him down on the table and let him finish the rest of the mac and cheese and my milk.

"Ah! What is that thing?" Eli exclaimed, pointing at Pinky.

"Oh, he's harmless. I found him at the vet clinic a few days ago."

"I see. Good to know he's not a wild rat. How long has it been since you've eaten?"

"About a day. We've been walking all night, so we're extra hungry."

"Where are you heading?" Eli asked.

"I'm not sure," I admitted. "I'm searching for some medicine while trying to avoid the Fates and the Furies."

"That is a good idea!" he exclaimed. "There is a small town a few days farther west on the same road you were on. They should have a pharmacy there. Speaking of medicine, do you have any pain pills? My ankle is starting to hurt again."

"Here you go," I said, handing him the bottle of aspirin from my backpack.

Eli popped two pills in his mouth and washed them down with the rest of the milk. "Do you think you could help me bury my wife and clean the smell of death out of this cabin?"

"Yes, certainly. Let me clean up the table and rest and catch a little rest." I yawned. "I've been up all night and don't have the strength to lift her now."

"I am a bit tired as well," he said with a yawn of his own.

"Yawns are contagious, aren't they?" I said.

He nodded, smiling.

I cleaned up as quickly as I could, stuck a chair under the only doorknob of the only door to the cabin, and went upstairs to the loft with my backpack and Pinky, leaving both dogs to sleep by Eli.

To my surprise, the quilt on the bed was soft and smelled strongly of laundry detergent. The thin mattress and cheap metal frame of the bed were more like a cot or something you would find in a child's room. The bed covered the entire loft except for a small walkway covered with gray Berber carpet. I lay down with my backpack at my side and closed my eyes and prayed silently so as not to disturb Eli. *Thank You, God, for a nice place to sleep and a new friend.* I fell quickly into a deep sleep.

*   *   *

Thunder roared in the deep purple sky as I sat on the hill of sand. Dread and fear threatened to strangle me as I started sinking. I wanted to scream, but my mouth wouldn't form the words. I tried to run, but my feet felt like lead blocks. A shadow man cackled in the distance as footsteps pounded the pavement, growing closer, ever closer, threatening to overtake me.

*   *   *

I jolted awake, a bit disoriented. *Just a dream*, I thought, relieved. *I'm in the loft at Eli's house. Everything is okay, and I am safe.*

"Lilly, wake up!" Eli shouted to me. "Wake up!"

"What is going on?" I responded groggily while descending the wooden ladder.

"I made breakfast." He smiled, motioning toward two bowls of oatmeal and glasses of milk.

"I thought you couldn't walk?" I said as I took the seat opposite him.

"I can't. Ice helped me move around. He's a good dog!" Eli petted Ice, and Ice whined and wiggled at his touch.

"He sure is," I agreed. "Yum, this oatmeal is good. I am so thankful you have food left."

"It's a blessing," Eli said.

I dreaded asking but said cautiously, "Where do you want to bury your wife, Eli?"

"I thought maybe we won't bury her," Eli said.

"How come? Aren't you planning on staying here?" I asked, gathering the dishes.

"No," he responded, his voice sad. "I want to go south and see if any of my extended family is alive."

"Are you sure that's wise? You are injured, and the Fates have been seen south of here."

"I'll give it a little time, but when my ankle has healed completely, I will set off to my sister Irene's house at night. She lives southwest in Grand Rapids by herself, and I haven't seen her since the Fates took over." He paused. "Besides, perhaps my sister and I will be able to find other survivors."

"But how will you get around here without Ice?"

"Look, I put two tennis balls on the front legs of this chair so I can roll it like a walker until my leg heals. I have enough food for at least a month. Don't you worry about me; I will be okay. You've got enough to worry about."

"All right," I said, tossing the aspirin bottle to him. "You keep these."

"Thank you," he said, setting the aspirin bottle on the table. "I will pray for safe travels for you."

"We really must be going now," I said. I picked up my backpack and Pinky and motioned for Ice and Puppy to follow me out of the cabin.

"Stay safe, Lilly. Good-bye in the literal sense—God be with you."

"God be with you, too, Eli," I said as he closed the door behind us.

The moon was still shining brightly enough to provide enough light for our journey. Eli had told us to go in the same direction as Jaden had. I hoped we would reach the pharmacy by morning.

"Brr, it's cold!" I exclaimed while picking up Puppy and placing her in my jacket.

She quickly fell asleep in my jacket next to Pinky, while Ice ambled on by my side. The cool, crisp night air caused me to shiver. *I need to call John*, I thought as I stopped walking to pull out and turn on the walkie.

"John, John," I called. "Are you there?"

"Hi, Mom," he said, sounding sleepy.

"Did I wake you up?" I asked.

"No, I'm just about to go to bed. I did the weeding today, and then the kids and I played baseball out in the backyard."

"That sounds like fun. Maybe when I get back, I can play too," I said, sorry I had missed the game.

"Sure, Mom, that would be awesome. We could play kids versus adults!"

"Not sure that's fair, but okay," I said.

"How are you, Mom?" he asked. "Did you find any medicine yet? Are you on your way back?"

"No, but two men I met told me a pharmacy is not far up ahead. I should be there by morning."

"That's great!" John said. "Are the men with you now?"

"No, as soon as one of them—Eli—heals, he will leave to find his family in Grand Rapids, and Jaden, the other fellow, is waiting at the vet clinic for his wife. I'll tell you more when I get home. I need to save the battery. I'll talk to you tomorrow."

"Okay. Love you, Mom. Bye."

"Love you, too, John." I switched off the walkie and returned it to my backpack.

We walked on in silence, listening to the whistling night air and the cries of unseen animals. As dawn approached, we came to the small town Eli and Jaden had spoken of. The familiar small-town welcome sign had been vandalized, spray-painted black over the name with "FATES" in red, with an arrow pointing southwest.

I wrote of it in my journal and marked it on the map of Michigan I was carrying while Ice ran ahead. I blew the dog whistle to call him back. Although the town seemed abandoned, I wanted to be safe. Ice came back and lay down quietly at my feet. I was tired. At the far end of the town was what looked like a small mom-and-pop pharmacy, still standing. Oddly enough, nearly all the other buildings in the town were burned out. I took Ice and Puppy into the trees and left them there.

"Stay," I commanded. Ice lay down and stared at me with his big black eyes. Puppy mimicked him.

"You quiet down and stay hidden too!" I whispered while pushing Pinky deep down in my pocket.

I walked slowly toward the building, very cautiously, sensing someone was watching me. Sure enough, a young man came out of the pharmacy with a double-barreled shotgun pointed at me. He was average size with dark black hair, green eyes, and pale skin, and appeared to be maybe twenty-five years old.

"Stop where you are!" he ordered. "State your business."

"I'm just passing through, looking to trade for medication," I replied, calmly raising my hands over my head.

"Are you alone? Are you armed? Are those your dogs?" He motioned the rifle toward Ice and Puppy. Ice, sensing I may be in danger, had run up behind me and began to growl, making him appear like an angry wolf.

Before I could answer, the young man shouted, "Call them off!" while waving the shotgun at Ice.

I blew the dog whistle, and Ice sat down, staring at the man. Puppy sat next to Ice, whining softly. The man lowered his gun. I saw movement from the pharmacy and noticed there were others inside.

"What do you have to trade?" he asked.

"Silver," I replied hesitantly.

It's okay. Stay alert, be smart. Listen to me, do as I say. I will make your paths straight.

"Follow me," he said. "We can trade." He motioned for us to follow him into the building. I picked up Puppy and cautiously walked behind the man. Indeed, the small white building with fading red trim was a pharmacy. There was no power, but the shelves behind the pharmacy counter were stocked with various medicine bottles. The sun shone through the main doors, providing enough light to navigate the garbage-filled aisles. Most of the other shelves were filled only with dust.

The man said, "This is my wife, Martha; my son, Jim; and my daughter, Ella. My name is James. I had to be sure you weren't one of the Furies. They burned this town out, leaving only the pharmacy, by the grace of God. They said we could stay and serve as a trading outpost. What is your name, and where are you from?"

"My name is Lilly, and I am from nowhere," I replied hesitantly. "I'm just passing through."

I didn't trust this guy James. He had a microchip in his left forearm, and only people loyal to the Fates would choose to keep their chips in. Everyone else had removed the government-mandated chips two years ago when the Fates took over.

James quickly covered his arm when he noticed my staring. His wife and children stood silently, staring at the floor in submission. Their pale faces, green eyes, and red hair led me to believe they were of Irish descent. Dirt covered their torn clothes and rough, dry complexions. The children's vacant, sad eyes grated on my nerves.

"Okay Lilly from nowhere, what do you want in exchange for the silver?" James asked.

"Thyroid medicine. All you have."

"I don't know what that is," he admitted. "Come on back into the pharmacy and show me what you want." He gestured toward the shelves.

Very cautiously, I followed James behind the counter and led him to the shelves stocked with thyroid medicine. Surprisingly, the shelves were fully stocked. I pointed to the bottles marked "Synthroid," "Cytomel," "Nature Thyroid," "Amour Thyroid," and "levothyroxine." This was enough medicine to last me at least three years. James swept them all into a shopping bag and handed them to me. I gave him the two bars of silver.

"Need anything else?" he barked.

"How about that book over there—*Pharmacopeia?* And some Zithromax, Bactrim, bacitracin, vitamins, chocolate, and water?"

"All that, eh?" James laughed. "What do you have left to trade?"

"A few bars of gold," I replied.

James raised his eyebrow, head cocked in disbelief. "No one around here has gold. Show me!" he commanded.

I put the shopping bag full of meds into my backpack and pulled out the three one-ounce gold bars I had brought. James looked at the gold bars in disbelief and said, "Anything else?"

Offer him the pickles.

"I have homemade pickles," I said with a laugh. "You want those, too?"

"Pickles? Oh, yeah," he said. "They just happen to be Ella's favorite. We are starving."

"Deal," I said.

James handed me the heavy leather book and began loading up the rest of the medications I had requested into a shopping bag as I started to lay out the jars of pickles and bars of gold on the counter.

Transaction complete, we said our good-byes, which were not cordial. I snatched up Puppy and hurried out and away from the pharmacy with Ice following me.

"God, loose Your guardian angels to protect us," I prayed as I jogged as fast as I could to get out of that town. Instead of leaving town the way we came, I circled the pharmacy and headed into the woods behind it. We stayed in the woods, heading southwest for an hour past the town, then walking west, parallel to it, for another hour, and then turning back north. I knew we would eventually have to turn east to get home. I just didn't want to risk having James follow me, leading the Furies or their commanders, the Fates, to our farm.

After traveling nearly twenty-four hours straight, I began to grow weary. "Stop," I commanded Ice. The position of the sun told me it was high noon. I needed to rest. Ice began to sniff around for food as Puppy licked my face and tried hard to get in my backpack. She was hungry too. There in the woods, beneath the pine trees, was as good a place to rest as any. I laid the blanket down on the ground and sat on it. Ice and Puppy sat next to me, expecting food.

"Okay, dogs, and Pinky, here you go." I scattered a pile of dried dog food in front of them and cut a plastic water bottle in half and set it down. I drank a full twenty ounces of water with a thyroid pill. I was too tired to eat. The dogs had long finished their dinner, gone to relieve themselves in the woods, and now lay down on the blanket with me.

"Bedtime," I said as I plopped my head on Ice's backside, using him as a pillow. Ice moaned in protest, then closed his eyes to sleep. Puppy curled up between us, closing her eyes with Pinky laying atop her, safely tied to my wrist.

"God, show me which way to take home and watch over us while we sleep," I prayed, and then I quickly drifted off into a deep sleep.

Chapter 3
Ruth

But this thing commanded I them, saying, Obey my voice, and I will be your God, and ye shall be my people: and walk ye in all the ways that I have commanded you, that it may be well unto you.

—Jeremiah 7:23 KJV

"Wake up! Wake up now!"

I awoke with a start.

"Now! Hurry!" a chorus of childlike voices called to me from a ball of blinding white light, desperately urging me to get up.

I stretched my eyes in the deep darkness, still weary and needing more sleep.

"Hurry into the woods," one of the voices shouted. "Follow us to the church; the Furies are coming." The figures, resembling children, appeared to run deeper into the woods, shimmering in the distance. I jumped up, panicky, and picked up the blanket, my backpack, Pinky, and Puppy as I gathered my things.

It appeared to be the middle of the night, and I followed them into the woods, struggling to keep up.

"Wait up!" I exclaimed as I followed the narrow path deeper into the woods.

"Hurry, this way! Down the road, through the woods to the church in the clearing in the middle of the woods," they whispered just loud enough for me to hear, in a singsong childlike way. I could no longer see them. Their voices seemed to be coming out of the darkness from all directions at once.

I stopped to put on my night-vision goggles and then ran full speed—well, it was more like a jog, as I frequently stumbled on sticks and overgrown brush in the dark of night. Ice disappeared in the distance, following the shimmering figures as I feared I was falling farther behind.

"You must keep moving!" The whisper was frantic now. "One foot in front of the other. Hurry! The Furies are coming! They are looking for her!"

I could no longer see Ice or the shimmering, white figures. They had vanished. Puppy whined and shivered as she peered into the darkness that lay ahead. The night-vision goggles enabled me to see a bit. I was thankful that Mike had given them to me. I heard Ice barking somewhere farther along. I ran faster toward Ice's bark until I arrived at a clearing in the woods. I leaned against a nearby tree, panting, and doubled over to catch my breath.

The night engulfed us in darkness. In the faint predawn moonlight it was still difficult to see more than a foot ahead of us. I could not see Ice, just endless rows of pine trees. I blew the dog whistle, signaling for Ice to return. He ran back to me wagging his tail, shaking, and pointing to what looked like a small house. Perhaps this was the church? *Maybe the children are already inside.*

I walked as quietly and cautiously as I could toward the small house in the middle of the clearing. I smelled smoke, as if someone had a bonfire or barbecue on a grill without meat. As I drew closer, I discovered it was indeed a church with a pastor's living quarters attached to it. I could barely make out the rest of the structure in the dark, although it appeared vacant.

I approached the living space and noticed a wicker rocking chair on the old wooden porch. The porch wrapped around and ended at the church's front door. The lights were out. Feeling the full-blown fatigue of travel, I plopped into the rocking chair, too tired to wonder where Ice or the children had gone or why children would be alone in the woods at night.

"Didn't anyone ever tell you it's rude to sit on somebody's porch without knocking on the door first?"

It was the voice of an old man who seemed to appear from out of nowhere but had in fact come out of the church and was standing directly in front of me. He was short in stature, clean-shaven, and had white hair with skin as white as snow, like mine. He held a hunting rifle at his side.

*   *   *

I must have dozed off, and when I jolted awake, fear-stricken, sometime later, the sun had begun to rise.

"Relax, Lilly. Zephaniah 3:17. You must be famished," the old man said. "Come inside and eat. Quickly, we have no time to spare." He motioned for me to follow him into the house.

"Where did your children go?" I asked.

"My children are grown and have been gone many years," he said, nodding. "You must have seen God's angels. I have been praying for you, Lilly. Sit down. Breakfast is ready."

He pointed at a chair at a round table for two. I collapsed into the wooden chair and set my bags on the floor next to the hand-carved oak table in the middle of the kitchen. Although small, the room felt strangely inviting with its wood-burning stove, a small metal sink, an older-style white refrigerator, and a microwave.

The man set a plate of cooked white potatoes, canned Spam, and a tin mug of water in front of me. As I began to eat, I noticed Ice had followed us in. He drank from a dog bowl and ate some dry dog food with Puppy. I trusted this old fellow immediately. He had a way about him, stern and loving all at once, confident and wise.

There was a living room next to the kitchen that was just big enough for a sofa and radio. The pale yellow walls were decorated with pictures of the man and a woman I assumed was his wife, a younger man and woman with dark skin and dark black eyes, and a black dog that looked like a wild wolf. The younger man and woman appeared to be siblings and of African descent, while the older gentleman and his wife were Caucasian, perhaps of European descent.

Eating only compounded my fatigue, and I struggled to stay conscious. The man continued to talk, although I couldn't comprehend what he was saying. I stared vacantly off into the distance.

"Lilly, Lilly!" he said. "Are you all right!"

My mouth wouldn't form words. "Help," I whispered. My body felt heavy, and I fell face-first into the empty plate.

The old man took my arm and pulled me up. "Come now, you can rest in my daughter's room." He led me to the back of the house. I fell onto the bed, and sleep quickly overtook me.

*　*　*

"Ahh," I moaned. My whole body was quaking as sweat streamed down my face. "Where am I?" I asked, confused, both burning hot and freezing cold at the same time.

The door opened. "It's okay, Lilly," the man's voice said, comforting. "You're all right. Just calm down."

"Here, take these." He handed me some water and two of the antibiotic pills I had gotten from the pharmacy. "You've been running a fever for days. Take these and you should start feeling better soon."

"I've been here *five* days?" I asked as I swallowed the antibiotics.

"Yes, you've only awakened to take medicine," he said. "You don't remember waking up?"

"No, only darkness. I'm still tired. Have I been taking my thyroid medicine?"

"Yes, I have been giving you those, too."

"The dogs? Pinky? Are they okay?" I asked, scanning the room.

"Yes, they're fine," he said. "I put Pinky in his ball, and the dogs are running around outside. I've been looking after them, too." He paused to wipe the sweat from my face with a cold cloth. "Rest a bit longer. I have some more chores to do, and then we will eat dinner." He shut the door behind him.

I noticed my bag was on the floor next to the nightstand. There was nothing else in the room. I drifted back into a deep sleep.

What should I do? How do we find the twins?

*　*　*

I stood in the back of a tiny room with only a black card table with three small identical boys sitting around it. They had pale skin, jet-black hair, and dark black eyes that glimmered. A circle of light materialized around them in a dark room. The boys were working together on a complicated puzzle and appeared to be reading each other's minds.

"Do you need my help?" I asked.

They seemed not to hear or see me.

I saw only woods. Frantically, the boys put the puzzle together, and another image formed—a purple circular maze in the woods. Suddenly one of the boys stopped and moved toward me. He gave me a piece of paper that had three lines of words on it. The words blurred on the paper, making them incomprehensible to me. I looked quizzically at him, expecting an explanation. He nodded and went back to working on the puzzle.

Is this where I will find the twins? Will I need help?

*　　*　　*

Suddenly I jolted awake.

I awoke to dog kisses. "Ice, stop!" I commanded. The kisses continued. Darkness surrounded me. I tried to push him off the bed, and he started to whine. His fur felt too long and a little too soft; his tongue was long, thin, and gentle; his body was leaning heavily against me; and he didn't have a tail.

"You're not Ice."

He whined and full-body wiggled.

"You're cute, though!" I turned on the light and looked at his tags. "Bubba! Aw, you are so cute with your little nub and longish black hair." His long body; lean legs; small, floppy ears; beady little black eyes; and long muzzle caused me to laugh.

He whined excitedly, then jumped off the bed and walked backward out of the room. That was weird. I had never seen a dog walk backward like that.

"Bubba, come!" the old man said. "Go outside now!"

The old man walked into my room. "My apologies, dear. He acts like a puppy."

"That's okay," I said. "I have a herd of dogs."

"My name is Pastor Stephen, by the way," he said. "How are you feeling today?"

"I'm better … still a bit tired, though. How long have I been here?"

"Today is the seventh day you've been here. I have dinner on. Come out when you are ready," he said, and he closed the door behind him.

Very slowly, I arose from the bed, pausing to stretch my legs and back. I rummaged through my bag for some time, finally finding the walkie. I really needed to call John.

"John, are you there?" I whispered into the walkie. There was only silence. "John, pick up the walkie!" I said louder.

"Yeah, I'm here, Mom. Thank God! I've been worried about you. It's been so long. I thought—" he stopped himself. "How are you?"

"I'm better now," I said. "I was sick for a week. I probably won't be home for at least another week. I was able to trade for medicine at a small pharmacy. I miss you, too, John. How are things at the farm?"

"Good," he said. "We are sticking to your instructions in the binders. We still have a lot of fruit and vegetables to eat, so that is good. Fire misses Ice. I'm glad that Mr. Tim and Ruby, his daughter, are here. Mike found a way to connect our fence with the neighbor's yard. He says we need to find more wood and some solar panels for electricity. I'm so glad you finally got some medicine."

"That's great news. I am glad you all are getting along so well. There is a solar factory to the northeast of us. When I get back, we could see about going there. Has anyone else come?"

"Nope, no one else. Are you sure more people are coming?" John seemed a bit doubtful.

"Yes, I am sure," I said. "You need to pray and listen more. You will see. Many more will come. I need to go now so I don't use up the batteries. Love you."

"Love you, too, Mom. Bye." The walkie clicked off.

As I put the walkie in my bag, I checked to ensure that all the medicine and the book were still there.

You can trust Pastor Stephen, Lilly.

Can I trust anyone?

You can trust Me!

Okay, point taken.

Something smelled delicious. Maybe ham. *Yum*, I thought as I turned toward the kitchen.

"Stop!" Pastor Stephen whispered. "Go back into the bedroom, take Pinky, stay away from the window, and be quiet until I tell you to come out." He handed me the hamster ball and shoved me toward the bedroom.

Before I could ask him anything, he put Puppy on the bed, motioned for Bubba and Ice to lie down inside the bedroom, and shut the door in my face. I peeked out the window from behind the curtain and saw James from the pharmacy approaching Pastor Stephen.

"Where is she?" James shouted angrily, waving his double-barreled shotgun in the pastor's face.

"Hello there, James." Pastor Stephen replied calmly. "Whom are you referring to?"

"Lilly!" he shouted. "The woman with the black dog, roaming in the woods."

"Nope," Pastor said, "I haven't seen anyone in the woods."

"You haven't seen a woman with a black dog and a puppy in these woods?" He scowled. "I've been tracking her since she left the pharmacy. I hear barking! You're lying, old man." James took a step toward the front door.

"You are not welcome on my property or in my house, James. That's Bubba, and he doesn't like you. I locked him in the bedroom for your safety. Be quiet, Bubba!" Pastor Stephen hollered. He stepped between James and the front door and continued. "Why? Who is this Lilly woman to you?"

"No one," he said, "and it's none of your business. Ash wants to find where she is living. He thinks she has more gold."

"Gold?" the pastor said. "Well, in that case, I wouldn't tell you even if I did know where she was."

"Come on!" James spat back at him. "You know I need this!"

"You are on the wrong side, son. Now leave!"

"I'm not your son! I'll find her myself!" James lowered the shotgun and stomped off angrily into the woods.

Pastor Stephen lounged in the front yard for a bit. He appeared to be raking pretend grass clippings and late-summer leaves. After he was satisfied that James had left, Pastor Stephen came inside and said, "Come on out, Lilly; James is gone for now."

"I knew I couldn't trust him," I said as I sat down at the kitchen table.

"There was a time when I could trust James," he said, shaking his head. "But now he's pledged his allegiance to the Fates. He does their dirty work in exchange for food and protection for his family."

Pastor Stephen brought in a big pot of soup and set it on the table. He ladled out portions for both of us, then prayed. "God, thank You for this food. Amen. I sure hope you like ham and potato soup. Eat up."

"I love ham and potato soup," I said. "Thank you."

As I began to inhale the soup before me, I noticed how fresh the ingredients were: milk, butter, onions, potatoes, and the glorious ham—natural ham, not the canned stuff. No Spam tonight. As soon as I emptied my bowl, the pastor spooned in some more. I ate until my stomach complained.

"That soup was amazing! Where did you get all those fresh ingredients in this day and time?"

He stopped eating and replied. "I have pigs, cows, goats, and chickens hiding in a barn in the woods, among various other supplies and foodstuffs. You seemed to need protein, so I slaughtered a pig."

"Wow, thank you so much for sharing, Pastor Stephen."

"Anything for the great Leokodia." He smiled, then continued eating.

"Not really," I said, shaking my head, surprised at hearing him speak my given name. "I'm no one special. How did you know my name?"

"God told me about you. You are much more important than you think. God says you will find her—my daughter Ruth. God says you will save the twins, who are my grandchildren." He stood up and began clearing the table.

"Oh, the twins! I have had many visions of them," I said, nodding. I joined him at the sink to help wash the dishes. "But … why me? Why not you?"

Pastor Stephen didn't respond to my question, but deep down, I knew the answer to it. Something had gone wrong between Pastor Stephen and his daughter, Ruth—perhaps a rift in the family, as sometimes happens when children reach adulthood.

We finished cleaning up in silence. He took the bones from the soup, threw them out the door for the dogs, and then sat down on the old gray terrycloth couch.

He motioned for me to sit next to him and then picked up an old photo album from the end table.

"Look, this is the day I married my beautiful wife, Anna. She passed from cancer when the kids were nearing the end of high school—before the world changed. In a way, I am grateful she didn't have to see Ash betray us all."

He paused as I looked at the wedding pictures in the crackly old album with yellowing pages.

"This is the day we adopted Ruth and her twin brother, Timothy, from Africa. Their parents had died from a mysterious illness that no doctor could cure. We were on a missionary trip, along with medical doctors and dentists. Anna just couldn't bear to leave them in the overcrowded orphanage, so we applied to adopt them." He pointed to a picture of Anna holding one tiny baby with curly black hair, dark skin, and huge brown eyes, while the pastor himself was holding an identical baby, except this one had a red ribbon tied around her head. The picture had been taken in front of a tattered brown medical tent in what appeared to be the desert; the sun shone brightly against the blue sky.

"They were so cute!"

"Yes, my beautiful Ruth and little Timothy." He paused to wipe a tear from his face. "I am hopeful you will find her soon. She is in grave danger and ready to give birth."

"What about your son, Timothy? He doesn't know where Ruth is?"

"No, he hasn't spoken to Ruth since she married Ash. Timothy never liked Ash and didn't want Ruth to marry him. Last time I spoke to Timothy, he was planning to bring his wife, Opal, and daughter, Ruby, over to visit. I pray they made it out of Detroit safe." He turned the page.

"Wait, stop," I said. "Where is that place, the camp in that picture?"

"That's Spring Hill, a Christian children's camp up north. Timothy went the summer of his tenth year, but Ruth didn't want to go that year. Why? Have you been there?"

"I think so," I replied while staring at the camp pictures of a large, familiar lake on the edge of a forest. "Wait," I said. "See this picture of Timothy and a girl sitting on that big log, holding hands with their backs to the camera? I think that is me with Timothy." I recalled the phrase "friends forever."

"Hmm," he said, nodding. "Maybe. Timothy never told me who the girl was he was holding hands with. He just said she needed him."

I sat in silence, striving to fight back the childhood memories I had fought so hard to forget, to get past. I remember being happy at camp, where I was free and finally escaped their torment for a summer and made a friend. It had hurt so much when the end of summer came and I had to go back home. I had so desperately wanted that summer to last forever.

Suddenly a dog's angry barking disturbed my thoughts, and I grabbed my gun.

"That's just Bubba barking," Pastor Stephen said, rising from the couch. "I trained him to alert me when the Furies are nearby. James must have sent them. Quick—you must hide!"

Pastor Stephen shoved an old recliner aside, knelt, and lifted a corner of the faded red carpet, revealing a trap door and concrete stairs that led down to a cellar.

"Okay," I said, standing up. "But I'm not so sure about this. What about the dogs?"

"I will send the dogs out into the woods." His voice was urgent. "Come! Here, you must take Pinky with you. If anything happens to me, Bubba will move the rug and tug on the string to tell you when the Furies are gone. He knows the drill. Hurry, dear, because if they find you here, they will take you prisoner. They will assume you are a friend of Ruth— and they take all of Ruth's friends to their torture camp. The Furies think we know where she is hiding."

Puzzled as to why the Fates cared about one woman and her babies, I gathered my belongings and descended the concrete stairs into the cellar below. There had to be more to the story that Pastor Stephen had told me. I decided I would press him more after the Furies left. The pastor closed the trap door, and I could hear him laying the carpet back down and placing the chair on top.

A moment later, I heard two other male voices, deep and gruff, talking loudly to each other. They were banging on the door, and the first voice shouted, "We know you are in there, old man, so open up!"

"Hold on," Pastor Stephen said. "I'm coming."

"Hurry up, Pastor Stephen," the second voice barked harshly.

"I'm coming," Pastor Stephen replied calmly, walking slowly and deliberately toward the kitchen door. He took an unusually long time to unlock and open the door, as if to give me time to settle in before they entered.

"About time," the first voice said. "Looks like we're just in time for lunch." I heard him sit down in the chair I had vacated earlier.

I heard the fridge door squeak as it opened and bang as it shut. "Soup's on," he said, obviously removing the leftover soup pot from the fridge and slamming it down on the table. I could actually hear the boorish man slurping up the leftover soup.

"You're such a pig," the second voice chastised. "You just ate a whole jar of pickles at the drug shop this morning."

"I'm always hungry," the first voice responded.

"Excuse me," Pastor Stephen said, and he cleared his throat. "Ben, to what do I owe the pleasure of your visit today? It can't just be a lunch call." His voice was calm and held just the slightest hint of sarcasm.

"Tread carefully, old man," Ben said. "Ash only lets you live because he thinks Asha will return to you."

"Her name is *Ruth*," the pastor replied angrily.

"When she bled for him, her name became Asha," Ben said, slamming his hand on the table. "Where is she?"

"I don't know—wouldn't tell you if I did, either, but I truly don't know. I haven't seen Ruth since she left with Ash after their wedding seven years ago."

"I don't believe you," Ben, the first voice, retorted. "What do you think, Simon?"

"He's lying," Simon, the second voice, grunted. "He knows." I could hear him stomp slowly over to the sofa and plop down loudly. "We should stay awhile."

"Good idea," Ben agreed. "We'll make a day of it."

"That's fine," Pastor Stephen said. "Ruth won't be back." I heard him open the door.

"Where do you think you are you going?" Ben demanded.

"Out back to tend to the garden. Make yourself at home. I've got nothing to hide." He slammed the door behind him.

I could no longer hear their voices. There was a cot to my left with a pillow and a blanket. Next to the cot was a tiny nightstand with a battery-powered lamp. To my right were cases of bottled water and assorted canned goods. I hoped I wouldn't be down there long enough to need to eat again. "Here, Pinky," I whispered. "Go run around in your ball." I placed the ball on the floor and let him stretch his legs for a while.

Might as well sleep, I thought. Quietly, I laid my bag on the floor next to the cot and pulled back the thin gray blanket. Hidden beneath it was a small pink book like a young girl's diary. I picked it up and lay down on the cot. I turned on the lamp, opened the journal, and began to read.

Title: High School Diaries
By: Ruth Smith

3:00 p.m. Monday: My Reason

Ash finally talked to me today! I'm not invisible anymore! What a great start to my senior year of high school. The whole cheerleading team wants to be friends with me now too. I sat at a lunch table with all of them. Ash invited me to the post-homecoming football game party on Friday! He actually chooses me over everyone else. I have this cute red dress I'm going to wear with a silver necklace and white shiny high heels. He's so handsome, athletic, and popular. I'm so insanely happy. My mom and dad said I couldn't go to the party. They said there would be alcohol there and no parents. I'll just lie and say I am sleeping over at a friend's house from church. Little do they know there will be drugs there too and that we smoke pot in Ash's car at school! It's not fair! My parents never let me do anything! I'm only allowed to go to church and school. It's like they don't want me to be free. I'm going away to school in the spring, and then I'll go far away from here! It would be so great to marry Ash! He is angry sometimes, but I am too! He is sad sometimes, but I am too! I love him so much, and I just met him. The more we talk, the more I find we are so much alike. Ash was adopted from

Africa too. I wonder if we were in the same orphanage together? I forgot to ask him. I feel so sad when I am not around him. I can't wait to see him again at school. I wish I didn't have to go to school, but my parents make me. My dad says I have to get a high school diploma. Tim is going to college. He is the golden child. I'm not smart enough. I'm not like him. It would be great to be a stay-at-home mother and have some kids.

6:30 p.m. Tuesday: Way of the World

Today at school was so boring. Failed another math test again. Dad will be mad at me when he finds out. I'm such a failure! I was so lonely today since Ash didn't come to school. I tried calling his house, but no one answered. Since Ash wasn't at school, none of his friends talked to me. It figures they don't really want me around. I'll have to talk to Ash about it tomorrow. I had to sit by myself again in the library. I don't even read or study as Tim does. I fell asleep and was late for my Spanish class. Oh well, I suppose Mom and Dad will be mad at that one too! I'm sure I'll have to do extra chores or something. They are too strict. None of the other kids at school get in trouble for missing or being late to class. I hope Ash is there tomorrow. I love him so much.

6:40 p.m. Wednesday: TIME

The school called Mom and Dad today, and now I have to do extra chores all month! They are so predictable and too strict! I don't see why they do this to me. How am I supposed to study if I am doing extra work? Whatever! At least Ash was back in school today. He wouldn't tell me where he was. Ash really seemed happy. He said we could get married and start a family when we graduate. He says he has an inheritance coming when he turns eighteen. That is so cool! My bio-parents didn't leave us anything. Today I had a free period in school, so Ash, his friends, and I went off campus for a long lunch. Ash drove in his red convertible to the Coney Island down the street, and he paid for me! He is such a great guy. His friends were nicer to me today. I think he talked to them. I wish school was over. I wish time would move faster!

7:50 p.m. Thursday: The Pop Cans

I was doing my homework after school, and Mom interrupted me again! Mom yelled at me to clean up my room and get rid of all the pop cans! Mom thinks she can yell at me because she is upset that she is dying from cancer! I am sad about it too. I want her to get better. It's not my fault Mom got sick, but she acts like it is! At least Dad said I don't have to do the extra chores anymore. Dad is actually being nice to me. When I finally finished my homework, it was almost time to go to bed. Looking forward to leaving this place.

1:30 a.m. Thursday: Sleep

I so can't sleep again. I had another dream that someone was stabbing me with a knife. Right before I died in the dream, I woke up. I'm not sure why??? Other than Mom's cancer, everything else is going well. Ash and I talk all the time. Today we left school early. He took me to a movie and then to dinner at Coney Island. I don't remember much of the movie! We have to leave school, since my parents don't let me date. I'm almost eighteen. I can't wait till we graduate and can do what we want. Ash wants to move to Tennessee. He told me his bio-parents left him 100 acres of land in a mountain valley somewhere. I can't remember the name of the town. That would be so cool to live in a warm state! We could grow our own food year-round and have animals. Mom and Dad don't let me have a pet, since we have too many farm animals already, they say. I am so tired. I wish I could sleep instead of staring at the darkness surrounding me. This is horrible. I'll try counting numbers or sheep!

11:00 p.m. Saturday: Homecoming

Homecoming was so amazing! The party after was fabulous! I've never been to a party before. We listened to music, smoked, and drank. My parents would kill me if they found out! I don't think they will, though. Tim won't tell on me, although he told me I shouldn't be hanging out with "those kids," as he puts it. I'm not sure why he doesn't like Ash anymore. Anyway, I love Ash so much that I wrote this poem about him.

Last Request

Master, will You help me?
> Will You rid me of my pain?
Master, will You love me?
> Even though I'm not the same,
> These words of nothing, no thought,
> Flow with sorrow, hatred bought.
Master, do You hear my cries?
> Or, to You, are they unreal?
Master, do not hide Your lies,
> 'Cause they hurt me more than what's real.
> Come now, uncover Your mind;
>> Happiness is so unkind.
> "Little one, I cannot change the tide,
>> For Your choices have come in.
> Altering desperate actions,
>> Would demolish all my Creation.
> Though how could I ignore
>> The changing time Love adores?"
> "Now see, my once beautiful Love,
>> Fading beyond the Sun,
>> Nature's cruel course,
>> Unwinding everything, undone,
>> Creating confusion, not endorsed,
>> Spinning You all around,
>> Smothered, underground."

Then, Master, can You help me?
       Can You help my soul return?
Master, can You teach me?
       Teach me how to learn?
Master, will You love me?
       Love me as I do mine?
Master, don't forget me,
       For that would be malign.

2:00 a.m. Sunday: Dreaming of Naomi

I can't sleep again! This time I had a wonderful dream. In it, Ash and I were married! We had a big, modern home with lots of land! I had just given birth to our daughter. I named her Naomi. I've wanted a sister my whole life. Sadly, I realized I was never going to get a sister. That's when I started praying for a daughter. I have been for ten years so far. It would be a dream come true. I hope this really happens. Ash has not mentioned having kids. I think I can talk him into having one. Maybe then my dad would approve of me. Maybe my mother will live to see her grandchildren. Perhaps then she won't be angry with me all the time. Maybe then my mom will love me like she loves Tim. I'm not perfect, but Tim's not either. It's so not fair! I need to sleep. If I miss church, my parents will just be madder at me. Oh well, at least I have Ash to love me.

Wow, these diary entries are intense, I thought. As I began to drift off into a deep slumber, I realized I needed to find Ruth as soon as possible.

A loud thud against the cellar ceiling jolted me awake.

"Simon, we need the information!" Ben shouted. "Don't kill him."

"Just giving him a little incentive to get him talking," Simon responded. "He knows where Asha is."

"Her name is Ruth," Pastor Stephen rasped quietly.

I realized they must have hurt him already. *God, keep him alive*, I prayed.

"Not that again," Ben demanded. "Tell us where Asha is."

"Ahh!" Pastor Stephen screamed. "I wouldn't tell you even if I did know." I heard a bang, a cracking noise, then silence.

"Now look what you did, Simon!" Ben yelled. "You knocked him out!"

"So we will wait till he wakes up," Simon replied obstinately. I could hear him plop down into what I assumed was a chair at the kitchen table.

"I'm calling Ash and telling him what you did," Ben said.

"So?" Simon grunted.

Beep, Beep, Beep.

"Come in, Ash," Ben said. "Ash, are you there?"

"What do you want?" a deep voice snarled.

"Simon knocked out Asha's father. He might be dead."

"Well, did he tell you where Asha is?"

"No," Ben said. "He claims he doesn't know where she went."

"Aahh!" Ash screamed. "I want my firstborn son, and the girl must die on the eve of the winter solstice." He paused, then added, "Kill the old man, then come back here to the base in Tennessee. I have other intel that she went west."

"Yes sir, roger that," Ben replied.

Then I heard static and a final beep as the line, which seemed to be a long-range walkie, fell silent.

"Finish him, Simon," Ben commanded.

"Gladly."

Three gunshots rang out: *Bang, bang, bang.*

Overcome with horror, I struggled to catch my breath. *No, no. No.*

"Bye-bye, old man," Simon jeered, adding insult to a mortal injury.

"Let's go!" Ben said. "Ash wants us back at base."

I heard footsteps and then the sound of the front door slamming behind the two savages. Then silence.

Finally I heard the swish of the doggy door and the moving of the carpet and chair. Seconds later, Bubba pulled back the string from the trap door, freeing me. I rushed up to the living room where Pastor Stephen lay dying, blood soaking his shirt and trickling from the corner of his mouth.

Bubba whined and lay down next to his master to comfort him.

"Lilly, go home," the pastor said, his blue eyes now dull. "My son Tim should have arrived at your farm by now. He will be expecting you to return soon. Tell Tim I said to go to the barn in the woods." He sighed.

"Uh … supplies and animals are hiding inside the barn for you. Please don't bury me. Just go. They will know you were here if you do. May God bless you and keep you. May His smile shine upon you and grant you peace …" Pastor Stephen gasped, gave me a final look, and took his last breath.

I sobbed uncontrollably as Bubba whined, licking the pastor's hands, hoping to wake him up. I fell on Bubba and hugged him for comfort, crying, "Why, God? Why do the good people have to die?" I banged my hands against the hard floor.

I am protecting him from what is to come. You must do as he says, as it is My will. You must find Ruth and the twins.

I dried my eyes on my shirt, went back down to the cellar, and picked up Pinky, Ruth's diary, and the food and water. Back in the kitchen, I blew the dog whistle to summon Ice. He came immediately with little Puppy at his side.

I gathered some dog food and the rest of the ham from the kitchen. While rummaging through the kitchen cabinets, I saw a hidden video camera. I yanked the camera out of the cabinet and realized it was still recording. I switched it off and placed it in my backpack. I walked outside with Bubba following, his head hung low, dejected, reluctant to leave his dead master's side.

"Come on, Bubba," I said. "Tim is waiting." I motioned for him to follow Ice, Puppy, and me. He perked up a bit on recognizing his brother's name and began to follow us home. We would be part of his new family. We would heal together.

I picked Puppy up, gave a final glance at the house, now Pastor Stephen's tomb, and then began walking toward home, to John and the others I had left, praying they remained hidden and safe. Bubba followed slowly behind us, whining and glancing every so often at the house he was leaving now far in the distance. Some hours later, all the dogs stopped deep in the woods. They sat in the dense grass under the tall pine trees and refused to move.

"What now?" I sighed. I dropped my backpack and Puppy and slumped onto the ground. Ice tried to open the backpack with his teeth. "Ahh, dinner?"

"Ruff, ruff, rrruf," Ice replied, triggering an all out howl from them all.

"Okay, shush." I opened the backpack, thankful that I had remembered to grab the dog food. I fed all three dogs and Pinky and set out a bowl of water.

"Ah," I exclaimed. "I forgot to take my medicine." Ice looked at me as if to say, "What is wrong with you?" I slammed a bottle of water along with Armor Thyroid capsules, which meant I wouldn't be able to eat for an hour. I really wasn't hungry anyway.

The sun began to rise, lighting up the morning sky. I lay down in the quiet woods, listening to the gentle sound of birds chirping and the dogs' steady breath as they lay beside me.

I couldn't sleep. My body felt heavy and weak, and my bones ached on the cold, hard ground I lay on. I put in my earbuds and turned on *Thru the Bible* and listened to a sermon by Dr. J. Vernon McGee. I knew I couldn't be more than four days from home—two if I didn't stop. At some point, to my surprise, halfway through one of the sermons, I fell asleep, bathed in the cool, fresh morning air.

Chapter 4
Make My Paths Straight

Trust in the Lord with all thine heart; and lean not unto thine own understanding. In all thy ways acknowledge him, and he shall direct thy paths.

—Proverbs 3:5–6 KJV

Wake up, Leokodia. Wake up!

W I jolted awake and was again surprised to hear my given name again. Lilly is the English-translated nickname for my given name.

"I'm up," I shouted into the air. It must have been the middle of the night. I stood up. I had slept at least ten hours. I couldn't see two steps in front of me, so I put on the night-vision goggles. All three dogs stared at me, wagging their tails. Fortunately, Pinky remained tied to my wrist, burrowed down deep in my jacket pocket.

You need to leave. Run home now! They are coming!

In the distance, I heard the rumbling growl of an engine. *Oh no, the Furies, Fates, or some other foe?* All were equally bad.

I snatched up my blanket, plopped Pinky into my pocket, grabbed Puppy, put on my backpack, and began to run home with Ice and Bubba at my side. For three straight days, we moved quickly through day and night barely stopping.

Finally we reached my farm. *Home.*

Feeling mortally exhausted and gasping for breath, I plodded up toward the gate, barely able to continue.

"Stop," a deep, unfamiliar voice commanded. I could feel the muzzle of a gun against the back of my head. "Not one step farther until you speak the word."

"Zephaniah 3:17," I said, panting, thinking, *I might not be able to make it one step farther.* I doubled over with hands on knees for a moment before rising and hobbling toward the gate the man had opened for me. As I limped inside, I saw a tall, muscular man with dark hair and brown eyes standing in front of me.

It's Timothy. He's here.

The man came up under my arm to steady me.

"Sorry, it's protocol," he said, flashing me a perfect white-toothed smile, oblivious to the fact that this was *my* farm, *my* protocol. He looked much older than he had in his father's pictures, stronger and heavy from the weight of his experiences over these last few years.

"My name is Timothy," he said as we neared the house. "What is your name?"

"My name is—"

"Mom, Mom, you're home!" John shouted.

He rushed over and hugged me, lifting me off the ground.

Timothy stared in confusion. "I'm sorry, I didn't recognize you from the family pictures."

"It's okay," I told him. "You did the right thing. I would expect you to question anyone who wants in as God commanded me to do in the beginning."

Timothy nodded and smiled at me. I felt as if I had known him my entire life. In a way, I had. The dogs ran in behind me, jumping and barking at John, wagging their tails.

"Ice, I missed you!" John exclaimed as Ice jumped into his arms for a big hug. He turned to me. "Where did you find the puppy and the other dog? Do they have names?"

"Puppy doesn't. Well, didn't. I've been calling her Puppy. I know, very original. I found her at a gas station. You may name the puppy. Here, take this guy, too. His name is Pinky. There is a hamster ball in my bag for him to run in. Otherwise, make sure his harness is tied down tight, or he will run away. He is domesticated and can't defend himself in the wild." I handed Pinky to John, my hands trembling, then began. "The other dog is—"

"—is Bubba," Timothy interrupted, bemused as Bubba jumped up excitedly on him, covering his face in gentle kisses, glad to have an old friend back.

"You were at my dad's house," Tim said. He turned to me. "Is Dad okay?"

I was dreading that question. As I turned toward Timothy to respond, my head began to spin and I fell; everything went black. Voices called to me, but I couldn't open my eyes. Someone was carrying me while John stood in front of me, giving orders.

"Tim, carry Mom upstairs to her room," John commanded. "Put her on the bed, then leave and close the door behind you."

Tim placed me gently on the bed.

"Wait, take off her boots," John said. Someone pulled off my boots. Then came footsteps, a door closing, and a wet tongue sloppily licking my face with stinky doggy kisses.

"Brody?" I whispered quietly, struggling to open my eyes.

"Mom, what's wrong?" John asked anxiously. "What do you need?"

"Water, root tea, and food." I struggled to mouth the words. John held my head up and held the mug of water to my mouth. I drank the whole cup and began to cough.

"You all right, Mom? Did you take your medicine?"

"No," I admitted. "I missed three days. I've been moving nonstop. I needed to get home. Where is my backpack? The medicine is inside."

"I put it in the closet," John said. He got up to get me some medicine.

I took my medicine with the rest of the water. "Thank you. I need to rest. In an hour, gather the adults and come wake me up. We need to talk." I shut my eyes.

"Okay, Mom. I love you. Come, Brody, Mom wants to sleep," John said as he walked out of the room, Brody in tow, and closed the door softly behind him.

"I love you, too," I whispered. I fell asleep seeing my son's shimmering blue eyes and feeling the tremendous love I had for him.

"Mom, wake up!" John said, shaking my shoulder.

"Has it been an hour already?" I replied groggily. I threw off my blanket.

"Yes, almost an hour and a half," John said. "All the adults are waiting for you at the kitchen table. The kids are outside playing."

"What about you? What are you doing?" I asked as I attempted to stand. My legs wobbled like jelly from three days of constant running. I wavered.

"I'm helping you," John replied, smiling as he put an arm around my waist to steady me. John helped me down the stairs and into the kitchen and guided me into a chair.

"Are you all right, Lilly?" Mike asked, eyebrow raised.

"I'm fine," I assured him. "Just exhausted and hungry."

"I'll get you some dinner," Sarah said. "We already ate." She set a bowl of apples and pears and a glass of water on the table in front of me, then went back to her seat.

"Mike, Sarah, Tim, I need you to go to your father's barn, Tim. He hid some animals and supplies there. You must leave out tonight and gather everything he stored for us. Return immediately."

"What about Dad?" Tim asked. "Should we bring him back with us?"

I took a sip of water before responding. "I'm so sorry, Tim. Please don't go to the house. The Furies killed your father, and they may return to kill you, too."

"How did it happen?" Tim whispered, tears running down his brown cheeks.

"The Furies came to his house, looking for Ruth. I was in the cellar, where your father had hidden me, where he had hidden Ruth. They—"

"Ben and Simon?" Tim interrupted.

"Yes, Ben and Simon. Do you know them?"

"I do. We went to school together. Traitors!" Tim shouted, furious, slamming his large fist on the table.

I nodded, continued. "When your father refused to tell them where Ruth went, they shot him. Your father's dying words instructed me to tell you to go to the barn in the woods for supplies and *not* to bury him. He also said we must find Ruth and the twins."

"That sounds like something my father would say. He must not have wanted the Furies to know where Ruth went. Lilly, did he tell you where Ruth is?"

"No, I don't think he knew. I have the diary Ruth kept when she was in high school in my backpack."

Tim stood up. "We need to go now. My father must have had a vision from God."

Mike didn't move. "And what makes you think the Furies won't be waiting there to ambush us? Looking for you? You said you grew up with them."

Tim replied, "Ben and Simon must think I died in the War of Detroit. Otherwise they would be aggressively hunting for my only daughter Ruby and me."

"You have a daughter?" I said, shrugging.

"Yes, you have not met her yet. She is outside playing with the other kids."

"I see," I said. "There was a War of Detroit?"

"Yes, there was." His voice was heavy with sadness. "We will have to talk about the war some other time."

I looked at Mike, who still had not made a move to get up. "Ben and Simon were heading to Tennessee, so I doubt they'll be the—"

"The ones to kill us," he said, sarcastically. "Got it."

"There's always that risk," I said. "I've been living it constantly for over a week now."

Sarah walked to the door. "Okay, so let's call in the kids and tell them the plan." As she opened the door, laughter and playful shouting drifted into the kitchen.

"Kids, come inside now!"

Clair and Elise were the first ones in. "Why do we have to come in early, Mom?" Clair, the fiery one, asked.

"Just wait," Sarah told her.

Clair pouted as she took a seat at the kitchen table. Elise immediately sat down in her chair, quietly, questioning no one. *She's a gentle one*, I thought, *which is why John fancies her.*

The boys came next, running to their seats. Finally, Ruby came sauntering in and took a seat beside Tim. She didn't talk and would not make eye contact with me.

Mike stood up and spoke, all sarcasm gone. "Kids, Tim, your mom, and I need to go out to get some supplies. While we are gone, you need to listen to Ms. Lilly and John. Okay?"

"Sure, Dad," Kyle said. "When are you leaving?"

"Now," Mike replied, as he pulled his coat off the rack by the door.

"We need to pray first," Jeremy said.

"Yes," Mike replied. "You lead us in prayer tonight, son."

Head bowed and eyes closed, Jeremy prayed. "Father God, please protect my mom, my dad, and Mr. Tim. Please bring them home safely and soon. In Jesus's name, amen."

"Amen," the rest of us responded.

"Let's go," Mike commanded as he picked up his bug-out bag; we each had one. Tim had brought one as well.

"Bye, kids," Sarah said, and then she turned and followed Mike outside.

"Bye, Mom, bye Dad; we love you," the kids said in unison.

Tim knelt in front of Ruby but still towered over her frail body. "Look at me," he said. "These are good people. They will take care of you. I love you, and I will be back." He picked her up and hugged her, rubbing her back as she cried on his shoulder.

She was a beautiful child with dark black skin; long, braided black hair; and big chocolate-brown eyes. Just so thin. After some time, Tim set her down. "I love you, Ruby."

He turned to lead Mike and Sarah out. Ruby sat back down, staring blankly off into the distance.

*   *   *

A few minutes later, Jeremy asked, "May we go to bed? I'm really sleepy."

"It's a little early for bed," I said, seeing that the sun had not yet set.

"We worked hard out in the fields and played hard all day. May we go now?" he asked, sounding dejected.

I sensed he was hiding something but decided to let it go and replied, "Yes, all of you, go get ready for bed and say your prayers. John is in charge while I am recovering. You will all need to help out more around here with the other adults gone, so get some sleep."

To my surprise, all the kids got up and headed upstairs to bed, including Ruby.

"Good night," they all said except for Ruby. She turned away and walked silently upstairs.

"Good night," John and I replied.

When the kids reached the top of the stairs, John whispered, "Mom, do you think Mr. Mike, Mrs. Sarah, and Mr. Tim will be okay?"

"What makes you think they won't be?"

"I don't know," he said. "I just feel a heavy presence, like something isn't right."

"The best thing we can do for them now is pray. Come here. Hold my hands; close your eyes." I prayed. "Father God, You are a good, good Father. Thank You for the many blessings You have bestowed on us and for Your continued hand of protection. Let no weapon formed against us prosper and bind up any who would harm us. Protect our friends on their journey and bring them home safe. In Jesus's name. Amen"

"Amen," John said.

"Do you need help getting up to bed, Mom?"

"I think I do," I said. "Thank you. You're a good, good son."

I stood up, still a bit wobbly as John again held me around my waist. We moved slowly up the stairs and into my bedroom, with Brody following close to us, herding us as shepherds do. He must have heard the word "bed." I sat down on the bed, and John hesitated to leave.

"What's on your mind?" I asked.

"Are you okay, Mom?" He was obviously worried.

"Yes, I just need to rest. It was quite a week. Please take care of the dogs and make some more root tea for me. You are in charge tomorrow. Don't wake me unless there is an emergency. You all can go hunting when I wake up." I smiled at him. "Sound good?"

"Sure does," John said, smiling back, relieved. "Okay, I love you, good night.

"Good night, my son. I love you too."

John closed the door. I rolled over on my side. Brody was right there leaning against my legs, waiting for me to fall asleep so he could go get into my red rocking chair.

"I love you, too, Brody. You're a good boy." I stroked his back as I did every night. I prayed, "God, tell me what to do and make it apparent. I will listen. Amen." I closed my eyes and immediately fell asleep.

* * *

"Ow, let me go!" Sarah screamed. The faceless man bound her hands behind her while repeatedly striking her across the face with his other hand.

"No, you're mine. You have always been mine! I will never let you go!" he shouted, pulling her away from Mike and Tim and heading toward his truck.

She scratched and clawed at him. He knocked her out. He dragged her to his truck with one arm and pulled out a handgun with the other.

"Leave my wife alone!" Mike yelled while running after them. Mike failed to see the gun in the stranger's hand, and the assailant fired three shots. *Bang, bang, bang.*

"No!" Mike screamed in agony as a bullet ripped through his shoulder.

*   *   *

"Ahhh, no!" I screamed, awaking covered in sweat.

The children all ran up the stairs and into my room.

"Mom, are you okay?" John asked. He was standing over me, his face contorted from panic.

"Yes. Quickly, children, hold hands. We need to pray." They did as I commanded. "Father God, please protect our friends and bring them home safe. In Jesus's name, amen."

I will protect them; do not fear.

"Amen," the children responded.

I quickly changed the subject, not wanting the children to worry. "What time is it?"

"Afternoon," Kyle answered. "We just finished lunch."

"I see. Well, have you been out hunting yet?"

"No, but can we go now?" Jeremy asked.

"Yes, all of you go," I said. "Please watch out for each other, and don't go past the lake. Take Ice and the two sleds with some baskets. Gather apples on the way home."

"Yay!" the younger kids and Jeremy responded.

"Listen to John," I said sternly. "Do whatever he tells you. Got it?"

"Yes ma'am," they said.

I turned to John. "Take the walkie with you, and be back by nightfall. Love you."

"I love you, too, Mom. Do you need anything before I go?"

"No, I'm okay," I said.

They all ran outside, chattering, as kids do, about who would take down which animal. Hunting would provide a much-needed distraction from the trouble looming over us and provide some food, too, as autumn was coming. I hoped they would get a deer. Some venison sausage and steaks would be delicious.

I noticed that Ruby had stayed behind and was sitting in the corner, stroking Brody.

"You didn't want to go, Ruby?"

She shrugged, still refusing to talk or make eye contact with me. She seemed to like animals, though.

"Let's go downstairs and clean up," I said. "I doubt the others did."

Ruby smiled—*Progress!*—and followed me down to the kitchen. Sure enough, five sets of cups and plates were sitting on the table. Without any prompting, Ruby began taking the dishes to the sink to wash them. I let Brody outside. Who knows when the kids last let him out. He immediately ran over to the other dogs, wagging his tail.

I found the root tea John had made sitting on the counter in a Mason jar. The tea was a blend of boiled and strained ginger, turmeric, thyme, and chives. I drank it, needing the refreshment. Ruby shot me an "Ooh, yuck" look of disgust on seeing what I had drunk.

"It's an acquired taste," I told her, "and it helps clean out my lungs and reduces inflammation."

Ruby didn't respond.

"I'm going to take a shower now. You may play with the dogs in the yard or sit inside and read a book. Today we finally relax."

Ruby smiled and ran outside to play with the dogs. Just then, Pinky's little head popped up from her pocket.

Good, I thought. *He has someone else to watch over him for now.* As I walked back up to the bathroom in my room to shower, I prayed that Ruby would talk again someday.

We usually shower only every two weeks. I had missed mine, however, and decided to take one now. The hot water quickly filled the small bathroom with steam, completely covering the little mirror over the sink. The bathroom had only a standing shower, toilet, and sink.

I turned on the iPod I hadn't used during my travels and began singing "Rescue Story" by Zach Williams, one of my favorites and the first song on my playlist, as the hot water washed me clean, relaxing me as though all was right in the world.

I continued singing as I dried off and got dressed, only I could now hear a child's voice joining in. Ruby had a beautiful singing voice—much better than my own. I stopped singing, content to hear her sing the song. *It's true,* I thought, *that music has a way of healing one's soul, especially for children.*

I switched off the iPod and walked out into my bedroom. To my surprise, Puppy came running at me, jumping and wiggling her entire body and whining. I picked her up and began stroking her. Brody was in his favorite spot on my rocking chair, sleeping. He glanced over at me, seeming uninterested, and went back to sleep. Ruby stood in the corner of my room as if she were afraid to let me hear her sing. I sat on the bed and motioned for her to come sit by me.

"Ruby, you don't have to be afraid. God has blessed you with an excellent singing voice, and I won't tease you."

Ruby stared up at me, smiling.

"Did you know that the puppy is not allowed in my bedroom?" I asked.

Ruby nodded.

"Then why did you let her in my room?"

After some time with her eyes down, Ruby whispered, "Her name is Snow. She wanted to come up and see you."

"I am glad the puppy finally has a name. Look at me, Ruby. It's okay. I'm not mad at you, honey. But we have rules for a reason. Snow is not potty-trained; she needs to stay outside or in the kitchen until she gets bigger and stops peeing on my floor. Look at me. Do you understand?"

Ruby looked at me for the first time and quietly said, "Yes." Then she went to pick up Snow to take her outside.

"Snow and Pinky are your responsibility now since they chose you," I told Ruby. "Those of us who understand animals know that animals, especially dogs, choose their people, not the other way around."

Ruby smiled as she left my room without another word. I heard her open the back door and go outside with the animals. I expected the other children to be back soon and decided to surprise them with the chocolate and cheese I had found. I unpacked my backpack and put the medicine in the safe hidden in my closet except for one bottle of thyroid medicine, which I left on my nightstand so I would remember to take it daily.

I carried the rest of the items in my backpack downstairs to the kitchen. I glanced in the living room and saw Ruby curled up in a ball on top of Brody on the couch. Brody didn't let anyone lie down on him. Ruby had a way with animals, much like me. She appeared to be sleeping.

Quietly, I got seven bowls out of the cupboard and set them on the table. I squirted some Cheez Whiz into each bowl and then added two chocolates, a Slim Jim, and a handful of seeds to each bowl. Everyone got an equal amount. Then I covered the bowls with cloth napkins so the kids wouldn't be able to tell what was inside. I set a spoon and a cup of water next to each bowl. The sun had begun to set, and the kids would be home soon. So I sat in my chair, head in my hands, with eyes closed, waiting in silence.

God, You have to help me. I don't understand. I don't know what You want me to do next.

Wait, my child, patience. Soon your path will become clear.

A loud bang and footsteps interrupted my thoughts.

"Mom, Mom, guess what?" John exclaimed.

"What?" I said.

"We got a deer!"

"Where is it?" I replied.

"Kyle and Jeremy are bringing in the meat," John said. "We just finished cleaning it and smoking the bones in the metal smoker outside the barn."

"Great!" I said. "Did you remember to gather apples on the way back?"

"Yes, we did," he said. "The girls left the baskets on the front porch."

Brody had woken up and greeted John, jumping frantically at the smell of deer meat, barking.

"Down, boy," John commanded. "Maybe I'll give you some bones later."

Ruby came into the kitchen and was sitting at the table, waiting for the others. John sat down in the chair next to her.

"How are you, Ruby?" John asked.

"Fine," she responded softly.

"She speaks," John said, smiling.

Ruby nodded and smiled back at him as the door opened again. The boys and girls came running in, carrying a quarter of the deer washed clean.

"Wow, that is a big one," I said. "Please put it in the fridge, wash your hands, and sit down at the table. I have a surprise for you all. I will cook some venison for dinner later."

The kids did as I said and quickly sat down at the table.

"Where did you leave the rest of the deer?" I asked.

"It's hanging in the barn," Jeremy replied.

"Good. After dinner, you will need to finish cleaning and smoking the meat."

"We will," the boys replied.

"So what is the big surprise?" Clair asked, staring at the bowl in front of her and giddy with excitement.

"On the count of three," I said, letting the suspense build, "lift the napkin on your bowl. One, two, three!"

"Ohhhh!" they all said, oohing and ahhing.

"May we eat it, Mom?" John asked.

"Yes," I said gleefully. "Let's all eat."

"Thank you," the kids said in unison, so happy because none of us had enjoyed any chocolate, cheese, or Slim Jims in the last two years.

"Where did you find the chocolate?" Elise asked between bites, "and is there any more?"

"At the gas station where I found Puppy—whose name is now Snow, thanks to Ruby. And, no, there isn't any more, so enjoy it while it lasts."

I watched the children enjoying their treats in silence. Brody was sitting at John's side, while the other dogs stood outside the sliding glass door, eyeing the snacks, mouths watering.

Brody suddenly bolted toward the back door, frantically barking as if to say "Emergency, hurry up, help!" We all sprang up from the table and ran outside, with Brody herding us through the door. The other dogs ran after us toward the gate.

In the distance, I could see headlights approaching. It appeared to be a semitruck with two passengers.

"They're back!" Clair proclaimed excitedly while running toward the gate.

"Hush, children, and stand back," I ordered. "I'll get the gate. I motioned for the dogs to sit and stay, and ran toward the entrance. As the semitruck approached, I could see Tim driving and Mike slumped over in the passenger seat. There was no sign of Sarah. My stomach sank, filled with dread, as I realized Mike was injured. The dream had come true.

"Kids, go stand on the porch and wait for us," I commanded. They did not need to hear this conversation or see Mike.

I opened the gate to let the vehicle in. Tim pulled up in the driveway as far up as he could. I closed the gate behind them and rushed up to the truck and said, "What happened?"

"Some of the Furies were waiting," Tim said. He looked terrible. "One of them, Seth, took Sarah. Mike got shot trying to get them to let Sarah go. We have to hurry, Lilly; he has lost a lot of blood, and he's beginning to fade. I patched him up as best I could, but we need to get him inside."

"John!" I called. "Come help us carry Mike into the living room and place him on the couch. Kyle, hold the door open."

"It's Dad," Clair shouted. "Is he alive?"

"Yes," I responded. "Please just stay calm, all of you, and pray."

John climbed up into the cab of the truck and took Mike by the shoulder. Then John and I took his left arm and leg, struggling under his weight, while Tim took his right arm and leg, and we pulled him safely down out of the truck.

"Ouch!" Mike groaned. His breathing was labored as we carried him in and laid him on the couch. The girls cried over their father while Ruby clung to her own father's legs.

"What happened?" Jeremy asked. "Where is Mom?"

"The Furies took her," Tim replied. "They were waiting for us. Your father tried to stop them and got shot."

"Is she dead?" Jeremy asked.

"They just kidnapped her," Tim said. He then added in a whisper, "As far as we know. As Ms. Lilly told you, just pray."

"Kids," I said, "go unpack the truck and bring all the supplies into the garage. Take the animals to the barn and give them each a stall next to the dog beds. If there is hay, lay some down for the animals. Also, give the animals some grain and water. The adults need to talk."

"Me too?" John asked.

"Yes, go now and help," I said. "I know you're an adult, but the kids need an adult to supervise them."

"All right," John said. "Come on, kids." He led them all out to the truck.

"Mike, seriously, what happened?" I asked. "No Furies were supposed to be at the pastor's house. How did they find you?"

"Well, Sarah lied," Mike said, his voice weak and struggling to breathe.

"Sarah lied?" I said. "Lied about what?" For a moment, I thought he was simply delirious.

He shook his head, sighed. "She didn't have her chip removed."

"What! She lied to us about *that!* She lied to *you!* Why would she lie? She is your wife and like a sister to me!" I felt so betrayed and knew that Mike did too.

"I guess she knew you wouldn't let us stay otherwise," he whispered. "She has low pain tolerance. She claimed her friends had cut it out, and I believed her."

"I don't believe that for a minute," I shot back angrily. "She wanted Seth to find her. She wanted to leave with him, and you know it!"

Mike winced. My words had cut him to the core. I was angry at him too, thinking, *He is just as guilty. He has been in denial all these years.*

Mike sighed. "She hadn't seen him for two years before the world changed. I thought she was over him. I was wrong."

"Too late now," I said. "The damage is done. Show me your arm."

Mike rolled over and presented his left forearm to me.

There was a deep scar where his chip should have been. I was satisfied. "What about the kids? I don't want any Fates or Furies showing up here!"

Mike shook his head. "The children were not required to get chipped, since they were all under eighteen. We didn't make them get the chips."

"Fine," I said. "Just rest, Mike. Tim and I have many things to discuss." I motioned for Tim to go with me downstairs.

As Tim led the way down to the basement, the old wooden stairs creaked beneath his weight. I realized Tim must have been at least six feet tall, as he had to duck going down the stairs, which groaned under his two-hundred-plus pounds of pure muscle.

I sat down in my old brown recliner, and Tim sprawled out on the beige loveseat. He looked at me intently as if he wanted to speak, but he did not.

"I have to ask, Tim," I said. "Are you chipped?"

Tim shook his head as he rolled up his shirt and showed me the scar on his left forearm. "No, I removed it myself after fleeing from Detroit. It's the same technology we used to use only in dogs. You know I was a vet."

"I suspected you might be a surgeon, seeing the great job you did patching up Mike. I forgot, but John had told me you were a vet. About the chip, I had to ask."

"Of course," he said. "I understand."

"It's just that I've known Mike and Sarah for years. I would never have thought they would lie to me about something this important." I paused to let the rising anger subside.

"Yes, that's a tough one," he said. "So what did you want to talk to me about?"

"Ruth," I said. "Your father said we need to find her and her children."

"What do you mean?" he said, rolling his shoulders, clearly confused. "Ruth doesn't have children, and I haven't seen her since she married Ash. I have no idea where Ruth has been living the last seven years, let alone where she is right now."

I leaned back in my chair, hands clasped over my belly. "Ruth was pregnant when your father was hiding her for a time in his cellar. Your father said Ruth ran off one night after the Furies showed up at your father's house about two months ago. He said she would have, or recently had, twins and that we need to find her immediately."

Tim rubbed a hand through his dark hair and sighed.

"Here, read Ruth's diary." I handed the book to him. "Maybe it will give you a clue as to where she ran off to."

He began to read it, making no sounds or movement. I sat waiting, looking around the room, wondering what would happen next.

Tim sat utterly still and silent as he read five pages before abruptly closing the book.

"So did any of that help you figure out where Ruth went?"

He nodded. "Yes. She is hiding in the lavender labyrinth we used to visit as children at Cherry Point Farm south of Silver Lake in Shelby."

"Shelby, Michigan? Are you sure?" I asked, leaning forward.

"Yes," he assured me. He paused before adding, "I should warn you that Ruth and I had a falling out before the world changed. I strongly opposed her marriage to Ash. She may not want to see me."

"Your father said she would," I told him. "He said her children would need you. I believe her children are the twins whose arrival God foretold me of. We need to save them. I overheard Ash talking with Ben and Simon on the walkie when I was at your father's house. He not only ordered them to kill your father but also said that he wanted his son back and would kill his twin sister."

There was controlled fury in Tim's eyes as he calmly said, "That explains why Ruth would finally leave him after all his abuse and manipulation, even though Ruth had vowed to Mother and Father that she would never leave him. Since we were kids, though, Ruth has wanted a daughter—wanted a daughter more than she wanted to live. Ruth must have found out that Ash intended to sacrifice their newborn daughter to his gods. I'm glad Ruth finally got up the courage to leave him for her daughter's sake." Tim shook his head, still trying to take it all in.

I stood up. "I think we need to wake Mike and review the video recordings I took from your father's house, to see if you can fill in some more blanks. It's time I knew more about these Fates and Furies."

Tim stood up too. "I agree with you, but we should leave Mike out of this—for now. He is weak, and when he hears what I am about to tell you, he will want to go search for Sarah immediately."

A chill ran down my spine. Legs still wobbly, I moved very slowly toward the stairs. "I need to get up to my room. The hidden surveillance camera I took from your father's house is still in my backpack."

Tim stepped up beside me and hitched his strong arm around my waist to steady me.

I shrugged him off. "I don't need help," I said. "I am fine."

"No, you're not fine," he said, refusing to let go of me. "It's okay to ask for help, Lilly." He guided me up the stairs toward my bedroom.

Tim had called me out on the emotional wall I had put up, had ripped off the mask I wore around men to hide my fear. There had been no need to deal with what had happened to me eighteen years ago—until now. I liked Tim. He made me feel at ease, safe, as though if I let go and trusted him for a second, the whole world wouldn't end.

Chapter 5

Answers

If any of you lack wisdom, let him ask of God, that giveth to all men liberally, and upbraideth not; and it shall be given him.

—James 1:5 KJV

The silence in my room calmed me. I hooked the video camera up to the TV on my dresser. Tim stood awkwardly in the corner by the bathroom as I sat down on my bed, TV remote in hand, ready to begin.

"You can sit on the recliner," I said, nodding toward my red chair.

"That seat's already taken," he replied, motioning to Brody, who was sprawled out across the recliner, head resting on the arm of the chair, asleep as usual.

"Brody, move!" I commanded. Brody got up slowly, moaning, and stretched before jumping off the chair and crawling under my bed—his routine.

Tim laughed as he settled into the recliner. "This is comfortable. I see why Brody likes it!" He reclined fully, his long legs extending beyond the footrest.

I pressed Play, and we focused our full attention on the video I had taken from Tim's father's house. The video started when I entered the hidden safe room in the cellar as Ben and Simon showed up at the pastor's house uninvited and unannounced. That explained why Pastor Stephen stalled before letting them in—he had to start the recording before they entered. I fast-forwarded the tape to the part where the men moved into the living room so we could hear their conversation.

"We need to convince Pastor Stephen to tell us where Asha is," Ben said. "Otherwise, Ash will kill us. We need to find Asha now! It is our last chance!"

"I'll beat it out of him," Simon replied with a sardonic laugh.

Tim's fists were clenched, and fury flashed in his eyes.

I noted that Simon wasn't as tall as I had expected. He appeared to be about five feet ten and two-hundred pounds, muscular, with dark hair and eyes, olive skin. He was possibly of Arabic descent. Ben stood about six feet two; looked to weigh one-hundred and fifty pounds; had pale white skin, black hair, and blue eyes; and appeared to be of European descent.

"Don't kill him before he confesses," Ben said. "Anyway, Ash wants him alive."

"Why?" Simon asked.

"Ash wants to make an example of the pastor—to torture him and then hang him on a cross to thwart any resistance to the Fates' regime." He grimaced at Simon. "You're so stupid."

"Watch out, or I'll kill you too," Simon said, scowling.

"That wouldn't be wise," Ben told him. "Because my sister, Number Four, will have your head if you harm me."

"Good thing your sister is a Fate!" Simon sneered. "She's your life insurance."

"Once we bring Asha back to the base in Knoxville, Tennessee, we will be promoted, maybe even given our Fury command army." Ben smiled. "No more being ordered around by that big oaf Jeffrey. We will be legends if we return her before the babies are born. That way the girl baby can be sacrificed on the winter solstice, thereby solidifying the boy's succession and power. The fortune tellers foretold this event years ago."

"I'd rather stay in the guard," Simon replied with a glint in his dark eyes. "I just want the spoils of war."

"You're a sicko," Ben replied. "The whole farm of women is disgusting!"

"Better watch your mouth, Benny-boy," Simon threatened. "I can report you and have you thrown in the hard-labor mines forever."

"Ash is aware of what I think about that. Just because I don't partake of multiple women whenever I want doesn't make me an enemy of the Fates. They can do whatever they want, as will I."

"What," Simon jeered, "are you a homosexual?"

"Nope. You know the penalty for that is death too. Number Three wanted to carry on the Middle Eastern tradition and made that rule early on."

"Easy there, buddy, I'm just messing with you," Simon told him. "No need to get all defensive. Besides, good old Number Four, your sister, would protect you anyway. And One, the Asian leader, seems to like you."

"Just shut up!" Ben shouted. "I hear the pastor coming back!"

At that point, I pressed the Stop button. I didn't want Tim to see his father die. I didn't want to see it, either—to relive the horror and start sobbing again.

I looked at Tim. His fists were still clenched, but he didn't seem shocked at all by what he had seen and heard. It was as if he knew what the Fates' final plan was. I had assumed it related to some demonic local presence, but this seemed to be much bigger, a global plan to bring about the end of the world, under the Antichrist.

"Tim, you said you grew up with these two?" I asked.

Tim looked at me. "I met Ash, Ben, and Simon during my first year of high school. We quickly discovered that Ruth and I were from the same orphanage in Africa as Ash was. At first he was the cool football jock. Kids flocked to him for his charisma, athletic ability, and stunning looks. As a freshman, he was the quarterback of the varsity football team. He was six-two, with light-brown skin and a muscular body, and he had unmatched agility—a phenomenal athlete, no question. Everybody liked him, especially Ruth. She had a crush to end all crushes on him."

"I picked that up from what I read in her diary," I said.

"Yes, before befriending Ash, the kids at school bullied Ruth daily, mainly because we were black and had white parents. We didn't fit in with either the white kids or the black kids. I didn't let it bother me and stuck to my studies. I tried to comfort Ruth through her depression, but I was never enough. I felt blessed to have amazing adoptive parents who brought us to America, but Ruth felt the opposite. She longed for our deceased biological parents—for someone, anyone, who looked like her. When Ash started to date her, the other kids welcomed her, stopped bullying her, and she quickly became the popular girl."

He paused and looked down at the floor, as if unsure of what to say next.

"What about Ben and Simon?" I asked.

"They were Ash's friends and teammates. Over the years, they became his bodyguards. They did everything he said. When he told them to jump, they asked how high."

I shrugged. "From what you are saying, sounds like they were normal high school kids."

"They were—until senior year, when Ash found out about his inheritance and heritage."

"Oh?" I said.

"On his seventeenth birthday, Ash received a letter from an attorney informing him that he had a huge inheritance. He was the son of a high-level human trafficker who made a fortune dealing drugs and slaves. His father, a black African, ran the ring out of Africa, and his deceased white mother was one of his father's former prostitutes. Ash changed after discovering the CIA had killed his father during an undercover drug raid. Ash never knew what happened to his mother."

"That was some heavy news for a seventeen-year-old," I said.

Tim nodded. "That is why Ash started getting into psychic readings and talking about revenge on America for murdering his family. For some reason, Ruth looked past all of that and loved him anyway. Ash wanted to unite radicals globally, and he began a blog focused on starting a new world order. I didn't think it would go anywhere. I thought he would get over his anger and move on with life. I thought we were safe in America. I was wrong." Here Tim stopped talking, leaving an awkward, heavy silence.

"There is no way you could have known," I said, trying to console him.

"True. I thought Ash was all talk. Mom and Dad and I all tried to talk her out of the marriage, but she was hell-bent on it. My mother died of cancer shortly after Ruth married Ash. It was odd that he wanted Ruth to change her name to Asha, but she went along with it. She didn't see that Ash was incapable of loving her in the way she needed. Ash was using her from the start. He fed on her desperation to belong. He wanted children, and Ruth always loved and wanted a big family. She must have been devastated to find out that Ash meant to sacrifice the baby girl. I am positive that is why Ruth left him. Pure evil." Tim shook his head and closed his eyes.

"Pure evil," I agreed. "Do you know Ash's end game?"

"No, I stopped talking to him in our senior year in high school. Even after he married Ruth, we didn't speak. Ash knew I disapproved of his actions and their marriage. My parents and I weren't welcome at their home. I heard from some acquaintances that Ash bought some land in the mountains of Tennessee somewhere near Knoxville. After the wedding, he hid Ruth away there and wouldn't let us see Ruth or speak to her. My father never told me about hiding her or having any contact with her. He must have been trying to protect my family." A single tear ran down Tim's face.

"May I ask what happened to your wife?" I asked hesitantly, not wanting to upset Tim further.

Tim sighed, eyes still closed. "I knew you were going to ask." He then began his story.

*　*　*

Day One: The War on Detroit

"Daddy, can I go play with the dogs in the kennel?" Ruby asked. "I'm bored."

"Sure, honey," I replied. "Mom and I are finishing up here, so don't take any animals out back."

"Yay!" Ruby ran off toward the kennels in the back of the building to play with the two small shelter dogs we had rescued and housed here.

"She's great with animals," Opal stated. "I think she will take up the family line of work."

I laughed and responded, "We have to get her through veterinary school first. It's hard work. I think she can do it, though."

"Sometimes I wonder about her," Opal replied while filling a syringe to give a rabies vaccine to the final patient of the day. "She seems to march to the beat of a different drummer."

"Here is Brownie, our last victim," I joked as I carried Brownie, a miniature one-year-old dachshund, to the steel surgical table for his shot.

The animal rescue we volunteered at was in the heart of Detroit, across the street from the Renaissance Center. It was a no-kill shelter called Little Angels that specialized in hard-to-adopt dogs. Opal and I volunteered there every weekend.

The shelter building was old and small. It had one room to attend to the animals' medical needs, a storage room for supplies, and ten or so kennels in the back. There were two entrances to the building. One door led to the main street out front, and the other door, located at the end of the kennels, led to the alleyway behind the building. This day was no different from any other Saturday.

The sun was bright, the skies were blue with no clouds in sight, and temperatures reached sixty-seven degrees Fahrenheit. Many Detroiters were walking around downtown, shopping, socializing, and having a good time. In the center square, a jazz band played upbeat tunes while people danced and swayed to the music. I hoped to go swimming in the creek behind our house later that day.

Opal interrupted my thoughts. "Good job, Brownie. Time to go back to your kennel." The small ten-year-old dog whined and shook nervously. "I know; have a treat." Opal gave him a small dog bone that settled Brownie down quickly. She carried him back to his kennel while I cleaned up the treatment room.

Ruby ran back into the treatment room, breathing heavily. "Mom said to tell you she wants to stay with the dogs a while. She said we could get lunch. I'm starving," she said, exaggerating.

"Really? Honey, do you want us to bring you lunch?" I yelled back to Opal.

"Yes, please. How about a grilled chicken salad with ranch dressing on the side from the Coney Island restaurant down the street?"

"Will do," I replied. "I love you. See you soon."

"I love you both too," Opal said.

"I love you, Mommy," Ruby replied as we walked out the front door hand in hand.

Ruby skipped along quickly, pulling me down the sidewalk toward our favorite restaurant, enjoying the warm summer day as she had done many times before.

Bang! Boom!

The buildings around us shook from a massive explosion.

Ruby began to scream. "Daddy, I'm afraid!"

I picked Ruby up and ducked into the nearest alleyway. "Shh, be quiet," I said, tapping a finger against my lips.

"I want Mommy!" she screamed, and she began crying.

I pressed her face into my shoulder to stifle her cries. Something wasn't right. I peeked around the corner and saw what looked like heavily armed police in riot gear marching down the main street. As the figures drew near, I realized they were not police. The army was some radical organization decked out in black body armor with patches that said "Furies." To my surprise, Ash, dressed in a dark cloak, was commanding them.

There appeared to be ten thousand soldiers, and they pulled people from the buildings and corralled those already in the streets as they continued to march down the main road before stopping in front of the Renaissance Center. Then the power went out in the surrounding buildings, causing the whole city to go dark and quiet.

"Attention, everyone. My name is Ash," said the familiar voice. "We are the Furies, and we are now in control of Michigan. I have military units taking over all the major cities in the United States. Your president is dead, and Washington, DC, is on fire. My three generals from the Middle East, Asia, and Europe are in charge. You will call us the Fates. They have taken over their respective continents. You will bow to me now," he commanded.

People began to murmur and complain. Some man in the crowd yelled, "You are a liar. I bow to no one other than the Lord Jesus Christ."

"Then you die today!" Ash replied, and the nearest Fury shot him in the head point-blank.

"Listen," Ash commanded as he turned on the radio. The broadcaster's voice quavered. "Run, hide, our capital has fallen, the president is dead."

Bang! Someone had shot him, and the radio went silent.

I scanned the crowd and saw my wife, Opal. The people around her quickly dropped to their knees on the ground, but not Opal; she stood firm. I pushed Ruby's head deeper into my shoulder, refusing to let her see what I knew was coming.

"Well, look at who is here today," Ash jeered. "Opal, and she's not kneeling with the rest."

"I will not bow or kneel to you, Ash," Opal responded courageously. "You are not God."

"I am God," he said. "And you will die." He shot her once in the temple, and she dropped and died.

"Furies, take these people to the Renaissance Center to be sorted," Ash commanded. "Shoot anyone who refuses to comply with my orders. Check the alleys for stragglers."

"Daddy, I'm scared," Ruby whispered.

"I know you are, love," I whispered, fighting back the tears. "We need to find a place to hide."

Ruby nodded silently. I carried her as we ran through endless dark alleys, heading away from the Furies, careful to avoid the garbage littering the walkways. After some time, I stopped to catch my breath.

"Daddy, we have to go," Ruby cried. "They're coming!" I heard their heavy boots pounding the pavement, drawing ever closer. I had come to a dead end. The Furies were behind me. I doubled back and turned right, beginning to panic as I heard the army coming from both directions.

"Down here," a man's voice whispered. "Hurry! The Furies will find you!"

I looked down at the ground and saw a man's hand poking up out of the maintenance hole below, beckoning us down into the sewers below the city. I bent down and handed Ruby to him and quickly descended into the darkness below.

"Be quiet," he said as he closed the sewer lid and locked it. He pointed to the wall for us to hide by, where a boy and girl stood quietly on the dank, smelly sewer floor.

I again covered Ruby's mouth with my hand as she shook, crying in the darkness. The sound of boots pounding the pavement above rang in our ears as I prayed silently for protection. Sometime later, the silence began to grate on my nerves. Ruby had closed her eyes and fallen asleep against my shoulder a while before, and the man and children had neither moved nor spoken.

"How long should we stay here?" I whispered.

"Maybe until nightfall?" he whispered back, shrugging his shoulders.

"Do you have any food?" I asked as I sat down next to the man and placed Ruby on the ground next to me, her head in my lap.

"Here, have a bag of chips and a bottle of water," he said, handing me the food. "We were on our way to Comerica Park after buying snacks at the liquor store down the street. By the way, my name is Lonnie; those are my kids, Justin and Elizabeth," he explained, holding out his hand.

"Thank you," I said, shaking his hand. "My name is Timothy, and this is my daughter, Ruby."

"How did you know how to lock the sewer covers?" I asked.

"It's my job to maintain the sewer lines for the entire city of Detroit, or at least it was. That's how I got tickets to this weekend's Tigers game. The city gives them to us workers every year," Lonnie explained.

"Amazing! I am so grateful God put you in our path to keep us safe!" I exclaimed.

"I am so grateful my wife stayed home today!" Lonnie said.

I began to sob uncontrollably.

"What's wrong, Timothy? Nothing to cry over. I'll show you a way out of the city safely," Lonnie assured me while patting my back trying to comfort me.

"They killed my wife, Opal," I said between sobs.

"Wait, so that courageous woman was your wife? I'm so sorry, brother; you got dealt a bad hand."

I sat there in silence and must have fallen asleep or passed out from emotional exhaustion, because sometime later I opened my eyes to find Ruby standing over me, shaking my shoulder.

"What's wrong, honey?" I asked groggily, attempting to stand up next to her.

Ruby didn't respond; instead, she pointed up at the sewer cover.

I turned to Lonnie. "Do you think it's safe to go up top now?"

"Well, I think we should stay down below until we get out of the city. There is no way to know if the army is hiding somewhere," Lonnie explained.

"I agree. You lead the way." I picked up Ruby.

"Come on, kids," Lonnie commanded as he turned on his pocket flashlight and shone it on the ground to light our way.

We followed Lonnie through the maze of sewer lines in silence for what seemed like hours. The stench of sewage and the sound of rodents made us hurry. Surprisingly, none of the kids complained; I thought they must be in shock from the horrific events of the day.

"Here we are," Lonnie said. "This one should open near the I-75 freeway." He climbed a ladder and uncovered the opening.

One by one, we followed him up into the night.

"Ha, I was right! We must leave now," Lonnie said. "Be safe." He turned and began walking south with his kids.

"Bye, and thank you again," I called as we turned north.

I picked Ruby up and began to run. I didn't look back until Ruby and I were far enough away to see the great city of Detroit burning to the ground.

*   *   *

"You see, Lilly," Tim said, coming back to the present, "it was a targeted attack. Cut the power, take over the world. We should have all seen this coming."

I nodded. "I know, Tim, I've felt something was amiss for a long time. I would pray, and God would tell me to get ready, though I never imagined a hostile takeover of America or the world. No longer the land of the free. It must have been difficult to travel up here to middle Michigan after witnessing the horror in Detroit—and while grieving." I shook my head. "So sorry."

"It was harder on Ruby. She refused to talk after we left Detroit. She misses her mother every day, and she doesn't fully understand why her mother died. She was five at the time."

We sat in silence, Tim on the recliner, I on the bed, contemplating what to do next.

After some time, I turned to Tim and said, "We need to talk to Mike. I need to know what happened in Bad Axe, and then we must go find your sister and the babies. We can't let that beast Ash get them."

"No, we cannot," he said. "Let's go wake, Mike. He's had enough time to rest."

As we walked in to where Mike lay, through the window I could see Ruby and the other kids playing outside. The aroma of the venison being smoked made my stomach growl.

"Mike, wake up," I commanded, nudging his good arm.

"I'm up," he said, slowly sitting up. "What do you want?" His face appeared peaked, his body weak.

"Mike," I said, "we need to know what happened in Bad Axe on day one."

He sighed. "I knew you would ask me about that soon." He paused and then began speaking.

*　　*　　*

Day One: Bad Axe

We were all at home in Bad Axe that weekend, as it was the first warm day in a while. Sarah was inside talking on the phone while she cleaned the house. I was outside in the shed, tending to the lawnmower, when Jeremy came up behind me begging, "Daddy, Daddy, can I cut the grass this time?"

"Can you handle the riding mower?" I asked.

"Oh, yeah," Jeremy yelled excitedly. His eyes sparkled, as this was the first time I had let him use the riding lawn mower on his own.

"Go ahead." Jeremy climbed up on the seat and cut the grass around the lot. He seemed happy to do chores, and I was okay with that.

I looked around the five-acre yard at the rest of the children playing as usual in the world they had made up for themselves, completely ignoring me. Our house was the American dream, with five bedrooms, four bathrooms with oak floors, a completely updated kitchen with high-tech appliances, and a finished basement. By the grace of God, we had finally arrived at our forever home. I decided to go inside and speak with Sarah. Today was the first Saturday I didn't have to work in many months, and I was sure she would want to spend time with me.

As I opened the door and began walking through the living room and into the kitchen, I could hear Sarah speaking with someone on the phone. I wondered who she was talking to. Before entering the kitchen, I stopped in the hallway and listened to her barely audible conversation. She sat at the table, happily conversing with someone.

"Ha ha, right! You are funny," Sarah laughed giddily into the phone.

"It will happen," a male voice responded. "You should take cover with us now."

"Yeah, right," Sarah replied. "Well, I don't believe you. Anyway, I have to go."

"Have it your way," he said. "I love you. Bye."

Sarah paused awkwardly, unsure how to respond, before finally saying "Bye" and hanging up.

"Who were you talking to?" I asked.

"Oh, that was my brother," she replied, refusing to make eye contact with me.

"What did he have to say?" I asked.

"Not much. I was telling him about the mysterious letter Lilly sent me—the one about how there is a war coming between angels and demons on Earth." She quickly changed the topic.

I let it go, as I didn't want to fight with her anymore. Lately that was all we did. I asked, "The letter telling us we could come to her house to stay if we needed to?"

"That's the one," Sarah replied.

"Have you talked to her about it?" I asked. "She seems kind of paranoid."

"I know. I was going to call her next week. The last time we spoke, she was upset with me, and I don't have the energy to deal with it." Sarah sighed. "Anyway, I just got done preparing lunch. Call the kids in, and I will set the table."

I opened the sliding glass door in the kitchen that overlooked the backyard. "Kids, lunch is ready. Come in now!"

All the kids stopped playing their made-up game and ran in immediately.

"What's for lunch, Dad?" Kyle asked as he sat down in a chair at the kitchen table.

Sarah replied, "Turkey sandwiches with cheese and mayonnaise, and chips."

"I don't like turkey," Kyle whined as he often did.

Sarah sighed. "How about a hot dog then?"

"Okay," Kyle said.

"I want a hot dog too, Sarah," I said.

"Does anyone want a turkey sandwich?" Sarah asked the rest of the kids in exasperation.

"We do," the girls replied in unison.

"Here, start eating," Sarah said, and she placed the sandwiches in front of Elise and Clair.

"What's to drink, Mommy?" Clair asked.

"I don't know. Ask your father!" She shot me a look and then continued to prepare the hot dogs for the rest of us.

"I'll get drinks," I said, heading to the refrigerator. "What do you want, milk or grape juice?"

"Chocolate milk," Clair replied.

"We want chocolate milk too!" the other kids shouted.

"That makes it easy!"

We all managed to eat and drink in complete silence—a rare occurrence in our busy household with four young children. Sarah wouldn't look at me and didn't speak. I wasn't sure why she had been ignoring me lately, but I was sure it would work itself out.

We had just finished lunch when a loud boom shook the ground beneath us.

"Ahh, what's happening?" Clair said.

Elise shuddered, and the boys just stared wide-eyed in silence.

"Go to the basement now!" I commanded, grabbing a flashlight and opening the basement door.

We ran downstairs and turned the radio to 350 AM, a local radio station near Port Huron, the closest major city. Three loud booms like massive bomb blasts shook the whole house.

"This is WJR radio 350 AM. We interrupt our regularly scheduled program for an emergency broadcast. Citizens in and around Port Huron, take cover immediately. We are under attack. The Blue Water Bridge has fallen. Again, take cover …" Then there was a loud bang, and shots rang out, followed by radio silence. A few seconds later, the radio went out, along with the basement lights.

"I'm scared," Clair said, crying and climbing onto my lap. The other kids followed her, tears streaming down their faces.

"What's going on? What should we do?" Sarah asked. She turned on the big flashlight we kept for power outages.

"We need to pray," I said. "I don't know what to do." I held Sarah's hand and began to pray. "Father God, protect us and lead us on the path we should travel next. Comfort us and give us courage. In Jesus's name."

We all said, "Amen."

The letter ... Read Lilly's letter.

"The Holy Spirit has told me to read Lilly's letter," I said. "I'm going upstairs to get it, along with a few more flashlights and some snacks." I gently placed Clair on the couch and pushed past the other kids and went upstairs.

Sunlight lit the upstairs of the house as I noticed the sudden silence. Not even a bird chirped. I found a few more working flashlights in the drawer next to the refrigerator. Along with the letter, I grabbed another bag of chips and some sodas, and I headed back downstairs.

"Here you go, kids." I tossed them each a soda and handed them the bag of chips.

I sat down on the sofa next to Sarah and said quietly, "I need to read Lilly's letter you've been telling me about."

I read it silently.

Dearest Mike and Sarah,

It's been a while. I know our relationship has been shaky lately. However, I have received a vision from God. God commanded me to write this letter to you. I am sorry if I have offended you or hurt you in any way. Know that I still care for you and your family. God gave me a vision. There will come a day soon when the world will change, and you will need help. Please come to my farm in Clare immediately. Your lives will depend on it. I pray that you believe me and listen to God's voice. Zephaniah 3:17. Burn this after reading.

Your friend,
Lilly

"Sarah," I whispered, "that letter is not as crazy as you made it out to be."

"Well, two weeks ago when I read it, I thought it was," Sarah said before adding somewhat sarcastically, "She's not always right, you know."

"Of course she's not," I said, shaking my head. "But she's not always wrong, either, you know? Lilly, is human, but sometimes she hears from God. We should go to her now. She can help us, and we are not prepared to survive in a war zone."

"I don't want to," Sarah said. "It's so far away. I don't think the kids will be able to make it there."

So I compromised. "Well, we could stay here for two weeks. We have enough food and bottled water to last us fourteen days if we ration it. Then, if the power is not on, we will have to leave."

"Okay," Sarah replied, deflated.

For some reason, she didn't want to leave.

She said, "Do you think we should we go into town and see if anyone knows what happened?"

"I will go alone," I said. "You and the kids stay here, hidden where it is safe. Don't leave the basement. I will burn this letter, too."

I said my good-byes and left Sarah and the kids in the basement. Before getting into my truck, I lit a match and burned Lilly's letter as instructed. I had about a half a tank of gas in the old black Ford F150, and I drove toward Rose's Diner. It appeared that our neighbors had lost power. No one was outside, and there was an eerie silence. Even out here in the country on weekends, people were usually out doing chores or kids were playing. *How odd*, I thought.

I arrived at Rose's Diner and Grocery Store. The lights were still on, and Rose's rusty old green Chevy Malibu was the only car in the lot.

Rose met me at the door and said, "Mike, hurry up inside. It's not safe." She waved me in and shut the door behind me, locking it and turning the lights off.

"Do you need something?" she asked, nervously peering through the window blinds, a stark contrast to her usual cheerful sunny disposition.

"I'm trying to figure out what is going on," I said. "We heard the bomb blasts, the warning on the radio, and the gunshots. Do you know what happened?"

Rose was a nervous wreck. "I heard too," she said, "and then I was visited by two strange men. They had on full-body black riot gear, with patches on both arms that read 'Furies,' with a red triangle with a white eye on the background."

"What did they want?"

"The Furies wanted to know about the area," she said, shaking. "Mainly how many people lived here, if this was the only store, and if we had a church. They were not nice men and threatened to kill me if I didn't answer."

"Did they do that?" I asked, noticing the handprint-shaped bruises on her pale arm suggesting someone had grabbed her upper arms and squeezed.

She nodded.

"I guess they were part of the attacking army," I said.

"Yes, they said the Fates are in control now and it is a new world order. The Fates will kill anyone who resists them."

I sighed. "Do you know where the Fates are now?"

"They took off in the direction of St. Peter's Church—to burn it, they said." Rose looked down and stopped talking.

"Where is John?" I asked. John was Rose's husband.

"They took him prisoner," she said, shaking her head. "They said if I continued to give them information, I could remain and keep the store open and they wouldn't harm John."

"What kind of information?"

"Mainly about the families living here, what types of supplies they have and purchase, how many people live in each house, the ages and sexes of those in each household, where the farms are, cattle, crops, and such. They want me to spy on my neighbors," she said, crying. "My own people."

"Did you tell them about us?"

"Yes, Mike. I'm so sorry. I gave them some information about the farmers—half-truths. You should leave before they get back. They've taken all the main roads and expressways, as well as the hospitals and gas stations. You should take your family and leave via the dirt roads and woods before they come for you," Rose warned.

"Anything else I should know?" I asked.

"They are tracking people by the microchips in their forearms, so I suggest you remove the chips before leaving."

"Could you help get this chip out?"

"Yes." Rose picked up a box-cutter blade and sterilized it in the flame of a candle burning on the counter. Then she poured alcohol on a piece of gauze and rubbed it on my arm. "This will hurt," she said before slicing deep into my forearm.

"Ahh!" I cried as she dug the microchip out of my flesh.

She dropped it on the floor and smashed it to bits beneath her feet. She poured more alcohol over the wound, which stung like nothing I had ever experienced, and proceeded to stitch me up with some thread and a sewing needle.

After applying a bandage, she said, "Here, take these supplies with you. One pill a day for seven days, change the bandage daily, clean the area, and apply Neosporin. I cut mine out as soon as the Furies left," she said while rolling up her sleeves to reveal a fresh cut on her arm where her microchip had been.

"Thanks, Rose," I said. "Take good care of yourself, and I'll pray for John's safe return."

"Hurry," she said. "You need to get Sarah and the kids and leave. Go somewhere else before the Furies return. Don't come back here or they *will* find you. I am leaving when you do."

I ran out to my truck and sped home to my family.

You must hurry. The Furies are coming. Go to Lilly's.

I hit triple-digit speeds on the way home, which was not difficult, because no one was on the road. I found Sarah and the kids all up in the living room, crying.

"What's wrong? Why aren't you in the basement? I told you to wait down there for me!"

Sarah refused to answer and looked away, still crying.

"Sarah, what is wrong?" I asked again. Silence. "Kids?"

Jeremy said, "Dad, some guys were here, and they tried to get Mom to go with them somewhere."

"Oh," I said. "Sarah, what's going on?"

"Nothing to be concerned about, just some friends trying to get us to safety. They gave us some food and medicine. It's on the counter in the brown paper bag."

"Listen up! We need to leave *now*. Rose said the Furies, an army of the Fates, are killing or enslaving people in Port Huron, and she said they would find us soon if we stay."

"Daddy, where will we go?" Elise whispered.

"We will go to Ms. Lilly's house. Hurry, pack some clothes. We need to leave within the hour."

The kids got up and ran upstairs to their bedrooms to pack. Sarah had not moved.

"Sarah, did you not hear what I said? Come on, get up and go pack and dress your wound!"

"What if I don't want to go?" she stated coldly.

"Listen, you are my wife, and I love you," I said, calmer. "It would be best if you came with the kids and me, and we are not safe here."

"Why, because Rose and Lilly say so?" she replied sarcastically.

"No, because God said so. He confirmed what Rose said, and God said to go to Lilly's farm."

"Fine," she said, conceding reluctantly, and went upstairs to pack.

"Wait," I said, "I need to cut the microchip out of your arm first. See, Rose did mine." I showed her the bandage.

Sarah spun around. "My friends already did mine, see?" She pulled up her sleeve and showed me the slightly bloody bandage beneath. Then she went upstairs without another word. I followed, wondering why she had been so sullen and distant lately. An hour later, we had piled into the truck with our backpacks of food, water, and clothes, and we set off for Clare, for the farm.

*   *   *

"And so we arrived here many months later. My only regret is that I didn't read your letter sooner. I believed everything Sarah told me." Mike stopped talking and looked at us.

I could tell he was tired and worried about Sarah. We all were. I didn't know how to respond, so I silently contemplated his story.

Several minutes passed before Tim spoke. "So, Mike, who are these friends of Sarah? Are they Furies?"

"One of them was the guy who shot me," Mike replied, wincing. "I don't know who the other men were. The kids interacted with the men a lot while I was gone. You can ask them."

Tim shrugged it off, turned toward me, and said, "Mike needs to rest. Let's go to the kitchen and talk."

In the kitchen, I began making myself a cup of root tea. "Would you like a cup, Tim?"

"No, thanks," he said, shaking his head and grimacing. "That stuff is disgusting."

"Suit yourself," I said, pouring my tea. I sat next to him at the table. "What are you thinking?"

"I'm thinking that we need to leave, Lilly. We need to find Ruth—and now Sarah, too."

"I agree," I said, drawing in a deep breath. "I was hoping to stay home until tomorrow night and recover a little more strength. With Sarah gone and Mike down, that's going to put a lot of pressure on John to manage everything while we're away."

He nodded. "He's a responsible young man, but I know what you mean. It will be hard on Ruby, too. I haven't left her since her mother died. But God will protect us and bring us back safe and sound." Tim took my small hand in both of his large hands, squeezed them gently, and looked into my eyes and said, "And I will help you."

After a few awkward moments, I pulled away from him and stared out the window into the moonlight. A lot of time had passed, and I wondered where the kids were.

"My turn," he said. "What are *you* thinking?"

"It's night," I replied. "The kids should be done unpacking by now, and I want to stay at least until tomorrow night to give Mike a day to rest and recuperate." I swallowed the last of my tea and got up and walked toward the door that led into the garage. Tim followed close behind me.

The kids were not in the garage, though it did appear that they had unpacked the truck entirely. The previously empty garage now held boxes of canned goods, baby formula, diapers, clothes, dog food, animal feed, hay, medical supplies, fishing rods, guns, ammunition, knives, gardening tools, water, water purifiers, survival books, a mill to grind wheat, a butter churn, a few sacks of chicken feed, and a multitude of vegetable and feed seeds.

I was amazed at the great volume of provisions Pastor Stephen had accumulated. "Praise God," I said. "He is so good!"

"Indeed He is," Tim said. "My father listened closely to God's voice." He paused for a moment as if observing a moment of silence for his father.

"He was a dear man," I said, remembering the ham he had prepared for me and how concerned he had been with protecting me. "He was blessed with a kind and generous spirit."

"Yes, he sure was," Tim replied. He stepped into the garage. "This food will last all winter or longer. Look at this." He stooped and picked up a document. "It's a map, from here in Clare to Shelby, where Cherry Wood is."

"Awesome," I said. "There's our confirmation."

"Yes, we need to go soon. Let's go find the kids." Tim walked back into the kitchen, map in hand.

This time I followed him, and we proceeded through the kitchen and out back to look for the kids.

A loud screeching sound broke the silence, and we heard Kyle scream. "Ahh!"

"What was that?" I shouted.

"The barn!" Tim shouted back. "Hurry!" He took off running to the barn, and I struggled to keep up with him.

We found all the kids and dogs surrounding Kyle.

Tim leaned down and wrapped a makeshift bandage around Kyle's arm. "There now," he said, his tone comforting. "You will be okay."

"What happened, John?" I asked.

"Kyle had a run-in with a big, bad rooster."

"Okay," I said. "Details, please."

John delivered. "We found a rooster and these chickens in the truck. We brought them to this stall and put them on a bed of hay for now. I was feeding them when Kyle decided he would tease the rooster. Not a good idea."

"Not a good idea at all," Tim said.

John continued. "Big Red lost his temper and clawed Kyle. We'll make a coop tomorrow. This book we found in the truck"—he showed it to us—"gives step-by-step instructions."

"You're going to live, Kyle," I said, "but please don't tease any of the animals anymore."

"You bet I won't," he assured me. "I'm sorry, Ms. Lilly, I won't ever do it again."

"John, you oversee the chicken coop project tomorrow. Elise, you will oversee feeding and caring for the chickens, pigs, and other animals," I said.

Elise nodded. "Okay."

"Now, come inside, everyone," I said. "It is late, and we need to eat dinner."

We all headed back inside except John, who lingered behind. I stopped walking and called to him, "Do you need help?"

"No, Mom." He stepped up beside me. "I need to talk to you."

"Sure," I said. "What's on your mind?" I hitched my arm around his waist.

"You're leaving again with Mr. Tim, aren't you?"

"Yes, tomorrow night. We *must* find Ruth and the twins."

"And Ms. Sarah, too?"

"Yes, her too. I hope and pray they are all okay. You will be in charge until Mr. Mike recovers. You're the man of the ranch."

He sighed and let his eyes close for a moment. "Mom, you just got back," he said. "And besides, I don't know if I can handle everything on my own and ..." His words trailed off.

"And what?" I prompted, eyebrow raised.

"And ... what if the Furies take you, too? I don't want to lose you, Mom." He was trembling, and tears streamed down his face.

"That *could* happen," I admitted, being truthful. "But you must have faith that God will protect us. I do. Pray for us without ceasing. I know you are ready to be the leader you were born to be, John. You have seen everything I did last year, and you have the guides and all the supplies from Pastor Stephen and farm animals now, too. You are more than ready."

"I know," John conceded. "It's just that I can't imagine life without you, Mom. You've always been here for me, and I love you." His eyes glistened with tears.

"Come here." I hugged him and held him tight. "It's okay to be sad and afraid, but it is *not* okay to let fear control you. Take authority over fear, cast it out, and give it to God. Pray daily. Sit in my rocker, under the weighted blanket with Brody, and ask God for help and strength as I have done countless times before."

"But I don't hear from God," John said.

"First, stop saying that; it's not true. Second, you must pray, wait, and be still. God will reveal the next steps to you. You must have faith. Mr. Mike and the children will need you."

"I will try, Mom," John replied.

"Don't try; *do*. I will pray for you, too, John. I always do. We will call home via the walkies when we can. I love you the most, my son," I said, giving him a final squeeze before letting him go.

"I love you more than most, Mom," he said. Then he turned and jogged toward the house. His athleticism still amazed me, as what came so easy for him had been a lifelong struggle for me. He was blessed and highly favored, and I have always said God made John from what was best in his father and in me.

"What was that about?" Tim said, when I finally caught up with them.

"Just encouraging my son," I said. "John figured we were leaving soon and didn't want me to go. He's worried. It's been the two of us against the world for eighteen years, and he's also a bit nervous about being on his own and in charge."

"I totally understand," he said. "Of course. John's still young. It will be my turn soon," he added, glancing toward his daughter. "Ruby won't want me to go either and will need a little encouraging."

"So let's stay at least one night more."

Tim nodded. "All right. I guess one more night will be okay." He smiled at me, and we stood talking for several minutes and praying God's favor on our mission and those who would remain at home.

When at last we entered the kitchen, we saw an assortment of foods on the table: carrots, venison, apples, and bread.

"Who set up this feast?" I asked. "I haven't had bread in a long time!"

"The bread and the butter were in the truck," Elise said. "It's yummy. It was Clair's idea to set out all these different types of food."

"Awesome, I haven't had butter in over a year," I said. "But where is Clair?"

"She took some food in for Mr. Mike," Ruby replied. "Daddy, come sit by me," she said, patting the chair next to her. Tim obliged and sat down, and I took the open seat next to John.

Clair walked in with an empty plate in hand and proclaimed, "Daddy is resting now. He is fine." Then she sat down and began eating.

I smiled at her. "Aren't you a good helper while Mom is away."

Clair smiled, and Elise added, "Mom told her to look after Dad while she is away."

How odd, I thought. *Why would Sarah make such a demand of her youngest child? Why not ask Jeremy or Elise?*

I didn't respond, as I didn't want to ruin the lighthearted mood. We all ate until we were full, knowing this would be the last supper before Tim and I would leave for what could well be many months.

After dinner, Elise and Clair cleaned up without prompting. The rest of us went into the living room. The kids sat on the floor, and Tim and I stood in the middle of the room, waiting on the girls to finish. Soon the girls came and sat down beside their brothers. Mike was awake but still looked a bit pale.

"Attention, everyone," I said. "Tomorrow night Tim and I will leave to find Ruth, Sarah, and the twins."

A bit of moaning and groaning filled the air.

I raised my hands to quiet them. "You all need to let us sleep late tomorrow. Make sure you complete all the assigned chores on the list in the kitchen before we wake up. While we are gone, and until Mr. Mike has recovered, John will be in charge. Any questions?"

"How long will you be gone?" Clair asked.

"We are not sure," I replied. "You all will need to follow the instructions in the binders for the fall harvest, finish the fencing, and hunt as much as possible."

"Do you think you will find Mom?" Kyle mumbled, eyes fixed on the floor.

"We will do our best," Tim said, "and with God's help, we will." Tim smiled, prompting Kyle to smile back.

*   *   *

After the kids went out to run off some of the feast before bed, Mike said, "How long do you think you will be gone?" His voice was thin and raspy.

"Could be months," I said. "We might not make it back until next spring."

He nodded. "Well, as soon as I get some rest, I'll take care of things around here—with John's help, of course. Don't worry about the kids. They are safe with me."

Tim nodded, and Mike managed a weak smile before lying back down and shutting his eyes.

"Tim, I'm going to go check out the farm animals and inventory the supplies," I told him. I picked up a notebook and walked out the kitchen door and into the night.

Tim sat down on the step outside and spoke quietly to Ruby. I knew she would miss him. At least she was speaking. Children's voices echoed in the distance in chilly darkness. As I strolled toward the barn, I saw the children running frantically around the yard.

"Hey, Mom, want to see the rest of the animals?" John asked.

"Of course," I said. Show me."

"Beside the chickens," John said, directing my attention to the stalls, "we have two goats, two pigs, and one milk cow."

"Good job housing the animals. Where did you put the hay and animal feed?"

"The hay is in the loft, and the animal feed is in the trash cans that used to have dog food in them."

"Good," I said. "Do we have any dog food left?"

"Yes," John said. "The two cans toward the front of the barn have dog food in them."

I nodded. "Great, so who wants to handle daily feeding and cleaning of the animal stalls?"

"I will," Elise replied.

Tim joined us in the barn, holding Ruby in his giant arms. "What about milking the cow and goat?"

"I will, Daddy!" Ruby said.

"Excellent!" I said. "A team effort! Follow me to the greenhouse. I need to show everyone how to maintain the aquaponics, as we may be gone a for a while."

I led them into the greenhouse.

"It's hot in here!" Clair whined.

"It is now," I said. "But trust me, you will be glad to have a warm place to play in winter."

"You sure will," John assured them.

"Is anyone allergic to bees?" I asked.

"No," everyone replied.

"Look in the back corners in the greenhouse, a few feet behind the orange and lemon trees. There are four beehives. Please don't go near them unless you have on a full beekeeper suit. The suits are in the metal cabinet to our right. Someone needs to collect honey every three months in these jars. Label the jars and store them in the root cellar. Then scrape off the honeycomb and store it in the freezer. There is a book in the cupboard above the stove that has all the details. Who wants to handle the bees?"

"I will!" Kyle volunteered.

"Awesome, thank you," I replied. I then turned toward the fish and continued. "The fish have laid eggs, see?" I paused to show the children the eggs. "I am placing this divider so that the fish and eggs are separated."

"Why do you separate them?" Clair asked.

"Because the fish will eat the babies otherwise. I need someone to feed the baby fish their flaky food, which is sitting up on the shelf right there. The adult fish get the cleaned worms from the cans. Once the babies grow to the same size as the adults, remove half of the adults and remove the divider. Then you will need to clean and smoke the fish for eating. A recipe and instruction book are in the kitchen cupboard above the stove to show you how. So who wants to tend to the fish?"

"I will," Ruby volunteered. "But I will need help with the cleaning and smoking."

"I will help her with that," Jeremy offered.

"Awesome! Thanks, you two," I said, walking to the row of high tables. "I need one more person to gather the tops from the root vegetables after cooking and transplant them in these shallow beds. Check on them every few days, and harvest the seeds they produce. Store the dry seeds in these glass jars and label the jars for use in the next growing season."

"I will take care of that!" Clair volunteered.

"Thank you, Clair," I said.

"Can we go to bed now?" Kyle yawned.

"Yes, we can," I said. "That's enough for one day. Let's go inside to bed." As we walked into the kitchen, I said, "Remember to let Tim and me sleep in tomorrow."

* * *

A few minutes later, I was up in my room, ready to lie down for some much-needed sleep. The dogs had other ideas. Brody, Bubba, Thing One, and Thing two jumped on and off my bed, chasing each other in a loud, playful manner. "Guys! Hush!" I shouted. "Bedtime!"

I lay down on my bed under my soft blue quilt.

"Urh," Brody responded while claiming the red rocking chair as the other dogs lay down at my feet and side.

"Father God, help us prepare for the journey that lies ahead. Heal Mike's body. Guide and protect the children in our absence. Lead us in the right direction. Amen." I fell quickly into a deep sleep.

*   *   *

The hot, dry air made it difficult to breathe as the sun glistened against the sand. Sweat dripped off my face as I followed the gigantic footsteps onward. Although I was by myself, I was not alone.

*   *   *

"Miss Lilly, wake up, wake up," a soft voice whispered.

"Ruby? It's late, dear," I said groggily. "Are you okay?"

"I had a bad dream," Ruby cried.

"Come here and lie down next to Bubba. What was the dream about?" I asked as I rubbed her back.

"My mom," she said, sniffling. "The bad people were hurting her, and then they got me, too."

"You're safe now, Ruby," I assured her. "We will all protect you. Your mom is up in heaven now with Jesus."

"I miss her so much," Ruby said.

"I know you do, and it's okay to be sad, but it's not okay to stay there. We must press on and finish the good work God has instructed us to do. Keep Jesus in your heart and make Him Lord over your life. Then one day in heaven, you will see your mother again."

"Okay," she said. "Is it okay if I sleep here?"

"Yes, honey," I said, and I tucked her in. "But tomorrow when you wake up, I want you to go downstairs and take the blank journal out of my desk drawer. Write all of your memories of your mom in there in remembrance of her. You don't have to share the book with anyone. Okay?"

"Okay," Ruby said, smiling. "Good night, Ms. Lilly."

"Good night, little one," I replied while closing my eyes.

Hours later, I heard Tim's voice whispering. "Ruby, what are you doing here? I've been looking all over for you."

Yawning, Ruby replied, "I had a bad dream. Ms. Lilly said I could sleep here."

"Come now," he whispered, motioning for her to join him at the door. "It's time to get up."

I lay there thinking for several more minutes while burrowing deeper under my quilt and shutting my eyes.

Wake up, Lilly! There is much work to do.

Fine.

I reluctantly crawled out of bed and dressed for the journey. The cool morning breeze blowing through my open window signaled the change of summer to fall. I added some warmer clothes, baby clothes, and my winter jacket to my bag. I had never unpacked the bag, which made things easy. As I walked downstairs to the kitchen, an old familiar smell wafted in, filling me with delight.

"Pancakes, Tim?" I asked.

Tim turned from the sink where he was washing dishes and said, "Yes, the mix was among the food from my father. Elise and John made them, along with bacon and eggs. We all ate, so come and help yourself."

"Yum!" I exclaimed while downing a full stack of pancakes.

"Slow down!" Tim said with a smile. "Have a cup of coffee." He handed me a mug of coffee and then sat across the table from me.

"Thank you! We've been so blessed. Thank you, Jesus!" I exclaimed between sips of rich black coffee.

Tim sat watching me eat. After some time, he said, "I'm sorry Ruby woke you up last night. She's been having a lot of nightmares lately."

"It's okay," I said. "I completely understand. Ruby can come to me anytime. I am sure she is sad you are leaving again. Where are the kids anyway?"

"Mike and the boys are outside setting up the chicken coop they found at the farm next door."

"So Mike's actually up?" I said.

Tim nodded. "I know. Seeing him last night, I wouldn't have guessed he could sit up, much less get up."

"That's good," I said. "John can use the help."

Tim said, "The kids also found wood, seed, and some tools, which John is organizing in the barn. The girls are downstairs, finding places to store all the food Dad left us. Elise also stocked the entire kitchen with food, including the cupboards and pantry. Praise God!"

"That is amazing! God is so good!" I exclaimed. "Where is the truck?"

"I drove the truck to the farm next door and parked it behind their barn, so it's not visible from the road. Maybe we could find a use for the metal bay."

"Maybe," I said. I thought about Mike again. "Do you think it's too soon for Mike to be up?"

"His body seems to be responding to the antibiotics, and he has more energy, although he's sad and worried about Sarah."

"Yeah, I knew he would be. Well, at least Mike can supervise the children while we are gone. I pray we find Sarah and Ruth soon!"

"Me too," Tim agreed.

"Did you pack a bag yet, Tim?"

"Not yet. I was about to pack when you came down."

"Could you add dried food, dog food, and baby formula to your bag?" I asked. "I couldn't fit any in mine."

"Of course," Tim said. "Which dog are we taking, and why?"

"Fire will come with us as a guard dog and warm blanket, as we may be gone through winter. She can also hunt small animals so we can save our bullets."

"Excellent," Tim said. "I didn't know she could hunt. Did you teach her?"

"No. One day before the world changed, she started bringing me small edible animals."

"Wonder who led her to do that?" he said, smiling.

I smiled back. "And once more wildlife returns to the ranch, I am sure she will do so again." I drained the last of my coffee.

"Want some more?" Tim offered.

"No, I'm full. We should take coffee with us tonight, too," I suggested.

"By all means," he said, pulling a jar of instant coffee from the cupboard. "I'm going to go pack now. I'll add coffee to my bag too."

After I finished my breakfast, John came in and invited me to go out and see the chicken coop the kids had been working on all morning. I was impressed.

"Wow! Great job, everyone!" I said several times as I walked around admiring the big chicken coop, which now stood right next to the grain fields and housed about twenty chickens.

"Eggs for days!" Kyle exclaimed.

I turned to Mike, whose role had been largely to supervise the coop-building project. "Afternoon. You look a lot better!" I noted that his complexion had returned to a normal color.

"No more fever, and I can't even tell I've got stitches anymore." He smiled. "A little sunlight probably didn't hurt, either."

I nodded. "I'm so relieved that you will be in commission while we are away."

"Oh, yeah," he said. "We should be able to tear down the barn next door and use the wood to start fencing in that house. Then we will clean the house and see how the electrical system is working." Mike advised.

"That sounds perfect!" I said. "We can check out the solar factory when we return."

Tim joined us a few minutes later and shared my delight with the chicken coop. "This is really fine work!" he said. "When I get ready to build my dream house, I know just who to call."

"Daddy!" Ruby ran up and jumped into her father's arms.

"Hi, honey," Tim said, effortlessly scooping her up.

Ruby planted a kiss on his cheek and, in a somber tone, asked, "When are you leaving?"

"When the sun begins to set this evening," Tim replied. He hugged her and set her down gently on the grass.

Ruby lowered her voice. "I don't want you to leave again."

"I don't want to leave either, Ruby," he said truthfully. "But we *must* find Aunt Ruth and Ms. Sarah."

"Why can't someone else help them?" she asked.

"Because if I rely on someone else, no one will help her," he explained. "You must be brave and do not fear, for the Lord our God will be with you and with me wherever we both go." Tim paused before adding, "And that means God will protect us, and we will be together in spirit."

Take the fruit with you too.

"Listen up, everyone!" I said. "I need help picking berries and fruit. Also, while we are gone, you will have to make sure to gather the outdoor fruit daily. Can any fruit you don't eat, and save the seeds."

"I'll oversee the harvest," Mike said as we began to harvest the outdoor fruits.

A few hours later, we arrived back at the house with many bags of fruit and growling stomachs. Elise offered to make spaghetti for dinner and insisted that Tim and I rest for the coming journey.

After dinner and kitchen cleanup, I gathered everyone and instructed them. "John is in charge, Mr. Mike will assist, and you all must listen to them and stay busy readying this place for winter. Remember to follow the preparation guides and pray for us."

A hush fell over the kitchen then, and in the silence I glanced sideways at Tim as it dawned on me again that I was about to embark on a journey, maybe for months, with a man I had known for only a few days.

Trust. Have faith.

The truth was, I didn't fully trust anyone on earth besides John. I prayed about it often; I prayed for emotional healing. But I wasn't there yet.

A little while later, Tim asked, "You did remember to pack all of your medicines?"

"Yes, I did."

"What else do we need?" Tim asked.

"Well, guns, ammo, diapers, and the baby carriers. I forgot to pack those, too. It's good you are coming with me this time."

"Why baby carriers? The car-seat ones or the ones for holding a baby on your stomach?"

"The stomach carriers, baby in front. We'll need our backs for the backpacks. We will each have to carry one baby."

"All right," he said, nodding. "I'll pack the weapons in my bag. You get the baby stuff."

"Sure," I replied, and I began packing. "God, please give me strength," I prayed out loud.

"Yes, and amen," Tim replied while packing the last of the supplies. "Something tells me we will need God's help daily as this will not be an easy trip."

* * *

An hour later, after saying our good-byes, Tim, Fire, and I stood out at the gate as Mike saw as out.

"Mike, be sure to follow the binder schedule and anticipate more people," I said.

"Relax," he replied. "You will have enough to worry about. We will be fine." He then added, "We will pray for you every day."

"Farewell," Tim said.

"Good-bye, Mike," I said as he shut the gate behind us.

Chapter 6
Faith, Hope, and Love

And now abideth faith, hope, charity, these three; but the greatest of these is charity.

—1 Corinthians 13:13 KJV

The sun had set as Tim, Fire, and I began our long journey toward the Lavender Labyrinth by moonlight. Even though we would miss the kids, I felt confident that John and Mike could take charge and lead them. John was the man of the ranch. He had grown into the man I had always hoped he would become—physically and mentally strong yet compassionate and brave—more compassionate and brave than I was.

We walked on through the moonlit night in silence for many hours, enjoying the cool autumn air. Winter would come soon, and I hoped to be back home by then with Ruth, the twins, and Sarah.

"What are you thinking?" Tim asked.

"That I hope we are back by winter," I replied.

"Hmm." He paused a while before adding, "But I'm not sure we will be."

"So we should keep walking and not stop for many breaks."

"So you will end up sick again," he said.

I didn't want to hear it, but he was right.

"I am a mighty man," he said, laughing, "but even I won't be able to carry you, Lilly, and the twins!"

"You are right, of course. I pray God will remove this crutch from me."

"Why are you in a hurry? Because you think we're going to miss God's grace?"

"If I didn't know better, I would take you for a preacher, Tim."

"I suppose that's what happens when you're raised by one," he laughed.

"You're not the typical PK—preacher's kid."

"That was my sister," he said.

"Your father was a wonderful man." I remembered his generous heart and kind eyes.

"He is," Tim corrected. "*Is* a wonderful man."

"Yes, he is," I agreed.

Some hours later, I said, "Do you think we should stop here, then, and sleep under the trees?"

"Yes, come on off the road. We don't want anyone to see us." Tim motioned me to follow him deep into the woods.

Fire had already found a spot in a clearing surrounded by trees away from the road we were following. She whined.

"What do you hear, girl?" I asked. She continued to complain and point at something in the dark. I didn't hear anything, so I blew the dog whistle and commanded her to lie down next to us. She obeyed.

"Who trained your dogs?" Tim asked. "They listen well."

"Before the world changed, there was a place just south of me that trained police dogs. I had them whistle-train Fire and Ice for protection. The other dogs are pure companion dogs."

Tim changed the topic abruptly. "Whom else did you send letters to beside Mike and Sarah?"

"Not many people," I replied. "Just my friends and family. At the time, I wasn't even sure why God wanted me to say what I did."

"And where is your family?" he pressed. "Why didn't they come?"

"It's just me and my brother and two sisters and their families. My mother and father passed some years ago. My siblings thought I was crazy and basically wrote me off. So I never really expected them to show up."

"Why not?" he asked. "So they do not believe in Jesus?"

"No, none of my family does. Or rather, *if* they do, they don't believe completely, meaning they haven't made Him Lord of their lives."

"I am so sorry," he said. "That must be difficult."

"At times, yes, but I will believe that they will come to Him until I meet our Lord God in heaven."

"That's some strong faith," he said. "How did you come about it—I mean, being in a nonbelieving family?"

"That is personal," I said, trying to close that door and lock it for now. "I really don't feel like talking about it."

"Okay," Tim said, "but it might help. I mean, I told you everything about me, and I know almost nothing about you."

"That is not true. You know I have a son, you know I am dependent on thyroid medication, you know God speaks and spoke to me about inviting people to my off-grid farm, you know where I live, you know my dogs, you know—"

"Yes," Tim interrupted, "but those are all things I can see, things happening right now. I'm curious, though. What is it about my past that leads you to think you can't trust me? I don't understand. You trust Sarah, who is untrustworthy."

"It's not you," I said barely above a whisper. "It's me." I began to cry. Fire began to lick my tears and growl at Tim, the one who had made her master sad.

Tim came over and sat next to me and began to rub my back. "I'm sorry, Lilly; I didn't mean to upset you. We don't have to talk about the past right now if you don't want to."

To my surprise, his touch put me at ease. I stopped crying and turned to look at him by the pale moonlight. I could barely see the silhouette of his face in the dark. To my surprise, my heart began to race anxiously. I hadn't felt this way in many years.

"How about we get some sleep?" Ice let out a low woof and lay beside me.

"Okay, good night, Lilly," Tim said as he walked a few feet away to where I could no longer see his outline and dropped down and slept. I pulled a blanket over me, as the temperature had begun to drop. Sleep came upon me as soon as I shut my eyes.

*　　*　　*

"Lilly, where are you? Lilly, help!" A woman's voice—a voice I had never heard—called out to me in terror, screaming. I couldn't see her, only deep darkness, and then a cold and sad feeling engulfed me as she continued to plead for help. My body felt heavy, as if I had iron weights pinning my hands and feet. Then fear enveloped me, and I wanted to scream, but my mouth remained shut. "Lilly, Lilly!" she cried. My fear grew until terror caused me to yell, and then …

*   *   *

"Ahhhh, no!" I woke up screaming in the hot sun, sweat coursing down my face—except it wasn't that hot, maybe fifty degrees tops.

Tim came running out from the woods. "What is it, Lilly? Are you all right?" He sounded worried.

"Yes, I am," I said. "I just had a nightmare. How long have I been sleeping?"

He shrugged. "Well, I've only been up for a little while. Fire and I have been watching you."

"That's creepy," I said teasingly.

He smiled, then turned serious. "You know what I meant."

"I do," I said. "Sorry, I couldn't help it. You left yourself open for that one."

"Touché," he said. "We had best get moving. According to this map, we need to go northwest, and I think we should loosely follow the road from within the woods. What do you think?"

"Well, I'm not that good at map folding or reading, but my compass says the road goes northwest, so I agree." I picked up the blankets and empty water bottles so we could refill them later from a stream if needed.

Fire sat looking at me, awaiting my direction. "Forward," I commanded, and we were off walking in silence, this time toward Shelby, toward the unknown. It was a bit overwhelming, but at least Tim was with me this time.

I am always with you, Lilly. Do not fear, for the Lord your God will be with you wherever you go.

Praise God. Where would I be without You?

Dead, I thought. *That's where I'd be without God.*

"Should we stop now?" Tim asked. "We've been walking a long time, and I am hungry."

"Sure," I said as I sat down on a log. "Here is as good as a place as any." Fire whined and began to dig at my backpack. "No," I commanded. She stopped, and I opened my pack and pulled out some water. I drank some and poured the rest into her bowl.

Tim sat down next to me and began eating a protein bar and drinking some water. "Are you hungry?" he asked.

"Not really. I just took my medicine and have to wait an hour to eat."

Tim looked away, then said, "So, tell me what happened to you and John on day one?"

"Not much until I noticed the power out in the town. We didn't realize anything was going on and thought that a car had hit a transformer or something."

"You didn't hear anything or see anything on the news?" he asked in disbelief.

"Nope." I shook my head. "I don't watch television—even the news—and on that day, I didn't have the radio on. You saw my farm—how isolated it is. The town is thirty minutes away, and the closest major city is about an hour. Detroit and Port Huron are a long way from Clare."

"Still, why doesn't John want you out by yourself? Did something bad happen?" Tim was prying, but skillfully, because his tone of voice and gentle manner put me at ease.

"You mean did something bad happen on day one or twenty years ago?" I asked.

"Both," he replied. When I didn't start talking, he said, "Fine, I'll settle for day one, but someday you will tell me what happened eighteen years ago—what broke you."

I looked at him and thought, *Doubt it*, but day one was a safe topic, so I took a deep breath and began.

*   *   *

Clare Day One

I sat weeding my modest vegetable garden as the sun shone upon me to create the perfect summer day. Birds chirped, the dogs chased each other around the yard, and I was the only one outside for miles. Our closest neighbor was a ten-minute drive away, and the town was about twenty minutes away by car. Peace is what I had wanted my entire life. *Praise God for this blessing of a homestead.*

The modest house was set on fifty acres just outside of Clare, a rural town in middle Michigan. At thirty-six, I had a home, some land, a greenhouse, a barn, and a garage for the first time in my adult life. Our electric truck was perhaps the greatest blessing we had received from God. *God is so good*, I thought.

Finally done, I stood up and began to gather the bags of weeds. We would have fresh beets, lettuce, cucumbers, and tomatoes in about two weeks. *Yum.*

John came running up behind me as Brody barked excitedly, wanting to play. "Hi, Mom, what are you doing?"

"I'm just going to put these weeds in the compost and change, then go to town. I must get my thyroid medicine refilled. Why?"

"I don't know, just wondered," he said. He still had a bad habit of being indirect with requests at seventeen, which drove me nuts.

"Well, spit it out; tell me what you want," I said, a bit irritated now. "I can't read your mind."

"Can I come to town with you and work out at the gym? I have to move onto campus at Central in two weeks and start intense workouts for baseball."

"Sure, I can shop while you work out," I said. "See, that wasn't so hard, was it?"

He smiled, shaking his head.

"Okay, let me change. You lock the dogs in the kitchen, and I'll meet you in the truck."

"Okay," he said. "What about Fire and Ice? Should I leave them out?"

"Yes, go ahead. Fire and Ice will be fine outside."

I went upstairs to change my shirt. I was so pleased with John. He had grown into such a handsome, compassionate young man. I was proud of him for getting an early signing decision on the Central U baseball team. He had been a state championship–winning high school state catcher and got an academic scholarship. Brains and brawn—so like me, only on some serious steroids.

He had seemed anxious lately, but I was confident that once he got to school and met his teammates, he would calm down and fit in as he always had. God had had his hand on John since before his birth.

"Mom, what are you doing?" John called from down in the kitchen. "I'm ready to go."

"Coming," I said while pulling a clean shirt over my head.

"Here, you drive," I said, and I tossed the keys to the electric Ford truck to John. On the way into town, I asked, "So, how are you feeling? Are you excited to move on campus?"

"Yeah," he said, rolling his shoulders. "But I'm going to miss you and the dogs."

"I'll miss you, too. Whenever you want to come home, all you have to do is call, and I will come to get you. It's not like you are hours away." I smiled.

"I know," he said. "But will you be okay by yourself?"

"I'll be fine. I've got the church, the dogs, and the garden, and I have friends. You can call me, too, of course." I smiled.

He pulled up in front of the family-owned gym that we had belonged to for years.

"What's the plan?" he asked.

"We can leave the truck here," I said. "Schmidt's Pharmacy and Grocers are across the street. I'll meet you back here in an hour."

"Okay, see you soon," John said as he headed into the gym. "Love you."

"Love you the mostest," I said.

"I love you more than the mostest," John said back, laughing.

I turned and walked to the grocery store, noting that the town was eerily quiet today. Not many people were in town. It was Saturday afternoon, but I figured maybe people had already finished their business and gone home. *Oh well, easier to shop*, I thought.

I went inside and walked the store aisles, just wasting time a bit, keeping an eye out for any sales. I picked up some ready-made Italian subs for dinner. *John would like that*, I thought.

It felt as if I had been there too long. I checked my watch; a half-hour had passed. In the checkout lane, I was surprised that I did not recognize the young couple in front of me, who were grilling the cashier about where the townspeople hang out on weekends. They creeped me out, though I wasn't sure why. I thought they were buying a lot of alcohol, and I assumed they must be out-of-towners here to party for the weekend ... or worse. I was sure I was just being paranoid.

"Hi, Lilly, how are you?" Beth, the cashier, greeted me with a hearty smile.

"I am well. How are you?"

Beth began scanning my items as she responded, "Happy to be off work in about an hour, as soon as Janet comes in."

"That's great," I said.

"That'll be twenty-two ninety-five," she said.

I paid by credit card, picked up my bags, and said, "Have a blessed weekend, Beth, and enjoy your time off."

"You too," Beth said, "and I will."

I went to the pharmacy next door, still unable to shake the feeling that someone was following me. I kept looking around but didn't see anyone.

You must hurry; they are coming.

I must have looked shaken, because as I approached the counter, Frank, the pharmacist, came out from behind the counter and said, "Are you all right, Lilly? You look a little frazzled."

"Yeah," I said, rolling my shoulders. "I'm just in a hurry. We've got to get home and pack John up for school."

"It's that time already? Summer goes by so quickly. John is going to do great at Central. Looking forward to baseball season."

There was something odd about the way he was speaking to me—too loud, as if for someone else's benefit.

I nodded and softly said, "Thank you."

"Anyway," Frank said, "here is your thyroid medicine." Frank was practically shouting at me as he shoved the bag into my hand. I went to pull my wallet out of my purse, but Frank whispered then: "No, you need to leave *now*, out the back door. John will be waiting. I called him. They are watching you." Frank motioned toward the back door with his head while shouting, "My wife should have dinner ready for you at Jane's down the street. Enjoy the rest of your weekend." Frank whispered as he again nodded toward the store's rear entrance: "Go now, take the dirt road out of town, and don't look back. God bless."

I wondered what was going on but suspected it was not good. I walked down the narrow aisle past undergarments for the elderly and durable medical supplies toward the back door. Sure enough, John had pulled the truck around to the back of the store and was waiting for me.

"Hurry up, Mom," John shouted, leaning over and pushing the door open. "We have to go now!"

I ran the last few steps to the truck and climbed in. "Okay, so what's going on?" I asked. "I'm so confused."

"I don't know either," John said as he pulled away from the pharmacy, driving toward the dirt road that would take us out of town opposite the way we came in. "Look behind us," John said.

"What is going on!" I exclaimed as suddenly there were about fifty people dressed in black riot gear pulling people out of stores and shoving them to the ground. "Shouldn't we turn back to help them?"

"Mom, what can we do? We don't have any weapons. We need to hide; we need to live."

As we turned onto the dirt road and headed out of town, two men jumped in front of the truck. John slammed on the brakes, and the men approached, waving machine guns in our windows. "Get out!" the one at the driver's-side window commanded.

"Okay," I said, "we'll do as you say." We got out of the vehicle and stood close together. "God help us," I whispered. John clenched my hand in fear.

Careful. Be calm, be brave.

He whispered, "What about your medicine?"

I nodded and whispered, "Shush."

"Shut up!" the first guy screamed, and he smacked John hard across the face—so hard his nose started bleeding.

"Ha, ha, look at the weakling," the man jeered. "Little boy's nose is bleeding."

"Do be quiet," the second man said. "Two is calling us back to town."

"What about these two?" The first man asked.

"Leave them," the second man ordered. "We got the truck, which is what Two wants."

"Fine," the first man said as he climbed into our truck. "Be thankful the Fates spared you today."

They turned and sped off toward town.

"Run, John," I said. "We need to run away now!" Five minutes later, I was out of breath. "John, wait up; I can't run anymore!"

He ran back to me. "Mom, don't stop! Hear those gunshots? We have to get home."

"I know," I agreed. "Let's walk through the woods. Are we even going in the right direction?"

John said, "I think we need to turn right here and go north when we hit County Road One, and then we are not far from home. Road One should take us to the dirt road leading to our house."

"Okay." I panted. "I'll follow you," I struggled to get the words out.

"Are you going to make it home?" John asked. "What about your medicine?"

"It's here, look," I said, pulling from my cargo pants the massive bottle of thyroid medicine, enough to last for a year, that Frank had given me.

"How did Frank know, Mom?"

"He's a believer," I said. "I think God warned him."

"Why save us and not the rest of the townsfolk? What is special about us?"

"He could only do so much," I said. "Who knows what helping us cost him. Let's just get home before dark."

We arrived home a few hours later. "I'm scared Mom. What now?"

"Let's try the radio." I turned on the radio but got nothing but static.

"That's odd," John said. "I'll try the TV." He turned on the TV and clicked through the channels. The same thing was on every station—that Emergency Broadcast System alert with the multicolored test pattern and a pulsing siren. A moment later, that faded to fuzz and static on every channel.

John shut off the TV. "This is not good, Mom; did the goons take your phone and wallet?"

"No, I hid them." I put my phone on speaker and dialed 911.

A recorded message came on: "The police are dead," the man's voice, deep and angry, announced. "Your government has fallen. Bow to the Fates or die. The choice is yours. We *will* find you."

I hung up, pulled the SIM card out of my phone, and smashed it to pieces. I handed the phone shell to John and said, "Take a hammer to this."

John went outside to destroy my phone while I rushed through the house, unplugging every electronic device connected to the internet and the modem itself.

When John returned, I said, "Where is your phone? We must destroy it, too!"

"It was in the car," he said, grimacing. "They have my phone."

"All right, don't worry," I said to reassure him. "It didn't have the GPS options enabled anyway."

"So what do we do now, Mom?"

"We pray and wait for others to show up. Today is the day God told me about nearly five years ago. Remember when our family and friends even made fun of me and called me paranoid? Well, I'm thankful I listened to God back then and listen to Him now. The others will come, and we need to get ready."

"Amen to that," John said.

*　　*　　*

I turned to Tim. "That's it. After that, we worked hard to scale up the crops inside and outside the greenhouse. That first winter was rough, but we made it through."

Tim nodded as he whispered, "God is good."

Then we began walking northwest for hours, largely in silence. *I shared enough for now*, I thought, and that had not come easy for me. The entire day had passed into night, and night into dawn.

"I need to stop and rest," I said.

"Good idea," Tim agreed. "Here?"

"Yep," I responded. I dropped my bags on the ground and lay down. "I'll eat when I wake; I'm sleepier than I am hungry." With Fire at my side and the sun beginning to climb above the trees, I took my medicine and then lay down and slept.

Hours later, I woke up. "Ow, Tim, stop it!" I exclaimed.

"You need to wake up, Lilly," Tim said, gently jogging my shoulder again. "You've been asleep too long. The sun is going down."

I propped myself up on my elbows, grabbed the bottle of water and protein bar he tossed at me, and quickly devoured both.

"Wow, I did sleep a long time."

"All day," he said. "You needed it."

"I do feel better," I said, stretching. "Though we really need to get moving. We have a lot of ground to cover."

Several hours later, I heard what sounded like an engine rumbling not far away. "What was that?" I whispered to Tim.

"Hush," he whispered, holding his finger to his mouth. "It's a car. Be completely still."

The car had stopped on the road close to where we were hiding in the woods. Fire growled, and I immediately blew my whistle, signaling her to lie down and be quiet.

"Was that a wolf?" a woman's voice said.

"Who cares?" a gruff man's voice responded. "We need to get back to the pharmacy tonight."

"Just wait a second," the woman said. "I need to finish my cigar first." They were close enough for me to hear her take a long drag on her cigar. "That sounded more like a dog anyway. You think someone is out there?"

"Doubt it," the man said. "We rounded up everyone from these parts months ago. I did see a white dog some miles back, though. Probably just a stray."

"Whatever," she said. "I'm done." We heard the car doors slam shut, and the car engine roared as they drove away.

"That was a close call," I said.

"Too close," he said. "We need to keep Ice closer. I wonder which pharmacy they are going to. Hopefully it's not in the same direction we are walking. Let's go deeper into the woods. Can you signal Fire to stay close?"

"Yeah, I just did," I told him.

We walked several hundred yards into the forest, away from the road, and headed north again. We walked in silence for hours, praying under our breaths that we would not cross paths with those people again. Fire stayed close until at last she sat down and refused to move. "What girl? Bed?" I asked. Fire looked at me, refusing to budge.

"I guess we stop here," Tim said. "I am not carrying Fire!"

We both laughed and sat on the ground next to Fire.

I gave Fire some water and food and then began to eat. Tim didn't say anything, just sat watching me.

"Are you hungry?" I asked.

"No," Tim replied. "I'm just thinking."

"About what?"

"About you," he replied.

"What about me?" I asked.

"Why you're so guarded," he said. "Why you don't trust me. I could have turned you in to the Fates many times if I had wanted to, while you slept in the woods. What happened to you?"

I didn't answer, just stared off into the forest, listening to the crickets' chirping and the running water from a far-off stream.

"You won't tell me, of course," he said.

"Wait," I said, quietly. "You don't understand."

"Then you could try to make me understand, Lilly." He was a gentle man, and his tone and manner were not at all threatening.

I said nothing for a while, just stared up at the sky. Then, feeling a peace about it, I said, "Okay I'll tell you, but you have to promise me two things." I paused.

"Fair enough," he said. "What are they?"

"First, let me tell the *whole* story; don't interrupt once."

"I promise," he said. "And the second thing?"

"You won't judge me."

"I'm not very good at judging people," he said, nodding. Then he looked me straight in the eye. "I promise. Go ahead and tell me your story."

"Thirty years ago, I was a completely different person. For lack of a better phrase, I was a hot mess. When problems or difficult situations arose, I tended to run away. Being forced to go to a Catholic school by parents who were not themselves practicing Catholics made me view the world negatively. I started to believe there was no good person in the world. I believed in and prayed to God, but I was not saved and had no victory. Devil worshippers cursed me in my teens, and I didn't understand why God would let this happen."

I paused, closed my eyes, and drew in a deep breath. A long moment later, I continued. "Those devil worshippers drugged and raped me in high school, which led me to become extremely depressed until one day I attempted suicide. I was fifteen."

I paused again and looked at Tim's gentle face and compassionate eyes as tears began flowing down mine.

Then I continued. "For years, I just kept running, trying to find meaning or purpose in life, only to be let down again and again. I'm not sure if the severe depression I suffered was from undiagnosed medical issues or just the pain of living. Probably both. But no one in my family even tried to help; they just kept saying, 'You're fine. Move on with your life.' But I couldn't move past the rape and got stuck."

"I met my ex-husband on an online dating app when I was in my late twenties. He seemed to care for me when no one else in my life did, and after two years, we married. My family kept telling me they didn't like him, but they never told me why. I was so used to my family putting me down and telling me I was wrong and shouldn't do things I liked to do or that I was crazy that I didn't listen and married him anyway. We were both practicing Catholics at the time, and I figured things would be good, or at least that he would take care of me."

I sighed, and Tim, keeping his promise, didn't say a word.

I continued. "The first three months of our marriage were good. I worked nights, and he worked days. Then I got pregnant, and it was the happiest time in my life. I had always wanted children. My dog Angel, a gorgeous white German shepherd, confirmed the pregnancy before even my doctor had. I knew that I would have a son because I had been praying for a son for more than thirteen years. As the pregnancy went on, my ex started drinking heavily and hiding liquor bottles throughout the house. He quit his job and became verbally and mentally abusive. I had to take a leave of absence because of complications due to poor health, lack of a thyroid gland, and the extreme stress my ex-husband caused me. After John was born, I passed out in the hospital as a result of blood loss and was ill for many months. I had some major health issues, which should have made it impossible for me to carry John to full term or killed me during birth, but God protected us, and we both made it through."

I ended my story and wiped my tears on the sleeve of my jacket.

A moment later, I looked at Tim and smiled. "Okay, that's it—that chapter anyway. You can talk now."

He nodded, looking serious. "How old were you when you got married?" he asked.

"I was eighteen, and my ex-husband was twenty-eight. I was at the lowest point in my life. I thought he would take care of me and love me. I realize now that he doesn't know how to love anyone, including himself."

"You were young, like Ruth. I see why God wants to use you. Ruth will listen to you. God is so awesome!"

"Indeed, God is," I agreed. "But there's more to the story."

"Please continue. I want to know all about you." Tim smiled. "I will go back into silent mode."

"You're a quick learner," I said, smiling. "But that was really only for the first chapter." I looked at his calm, dark eyes and huge smile that made me feel at ease. "The abuse continued to escalate, becoming even more physical on top of the mental abuse. One time he forced me to eat scalding hot food, and another time, he pulled me off the couch by my hair and I hit my head on the table."

I swatted at a tear. "In the meantime, John was diagnosed with failure to thrive and had severe acid reflux. I had cared for children my entire life and knew something was wrong. I was at work all night, and my ex was with him. I kept begging my ex-husband to get help, to go to therapy or Alcoholics Anonymous, but he refused to go and became more abusive. He had recently gotten a job as a contract worker, and one day when I got home from work, he had a bunch of his guns and rifles on the table and was loading them into a duffel bag. He was on the phone with his manager, arguing about something and slurring threats. After he hung up, he continued packing the loaded guns into the bag and, half-drunk, inadvertently shot a hole through the kitchen floor. Somehow, I managed to talk him down, and he passed out in the living room. I was terrified. I knew I had to get John and myself out, but I was too weak to leave on my own. That day I prayed for God to unblind my eyes and help us get out safe."

I hung my head then, ashamed of what I had let happen.

"What about your family?" Tim said. "Even with Baby John here, they didn't they help you?"

"My ex-husband wouldn't let me talk to my family, and he even threatened to kill them every time I brought them up or wanted to go see them."

"Wow, that must have been so rough," he said, shaking his head. "So how did God get you out?"

"A few weeks later, I was supposed to go out to lunch with the only friend he let me talk to and take John, who was eleven months old at the time, with me. Before Emily showed up, my ex-husband held a loaded shotgun to my head and told me that he would kill my mother and me if I ever left him. He seemed both high and drunk, though I wasn't sure since I had worked the night before and had just woken up an hour earlier. I was gathering John's baby stuff when my friend arrived. My ex-husband almost did not let me take John, and he followed us to Emily's car. Once we left, I started crying and told her everything that had happened. She forced me to go to the police, which started the hardest part of my life."

I was sobbing then, crying uncontrollably, as the wave of hidden emotions surfaced like a tidal wave.

Tim put his arm around me. "It's okay," he said. "That is your past, not your future. I am thankful God saved you both."

After some time, I managed to stop crying and said, "I am thankful too. It was hard because my ex-husband fought me in court for many years over John's therapy sessions and his desire to play baseball. He walked in and out of John's life, attempting to keep John under lock and key when John was with him and completely ignoring him for months on end when John was with me. The lefty judge let him do whatever he wanted and retain custody even though he had a felony and was on probation for the gun incident. Finally, after years of prayer and asking God to intervene, the Holy Spirit spoke to me. The Holy Spirit said, 'It is finished.' About three weeks later, my ex-husband got drunk in front of John and threatened his new wife, John's stepmother, which led John to tell his Christian therapist about it and refuse to go home with his father after school. The outcome was not what I wanted, as Child Protective Services would not rescind my ex's custody. Instead they gave all the power to John. They wrote a very detailed order allowing John to decide if he wanted to see his father, allowing John to play sports and continue therapy—all things my ex-husband had fought me on in court for many years. The last time John saw his father was when he was in fourth grade."

"Wow, I would have never known any of that," Tim said. "God has healed you and John. You don't strike me as people who went through all that."

"I hear that," I said, "but I have court papers to prove it. I assure you I didn't change or get better independently. During those ten-plus long years, I gave my life to Christ. I was saved and dedicated John to the Lord. I had the help of my small group at church during that time, most of whom were church elders except for Mike and Sarah."

"Ah," Tim said. "You met Mike and Sarah at church."

"Yes, I met them at church and became friends with them. One of the elders had God's wisdom and foresight to pray to break the curse over me, and I became partially free for the first time in my life. I spent long hours praying, studying the Bible, volunteering at church, and waiting for God to change me and the present circumstances. My faith grew over time. Although difficult at times, I've learned that waiting on God always produces the best outcome. Six years later, God delivered me." I smiled.

Tim's whole face smiled with me. "Amen to that. You must share your message with Ruth when we find her. Your lives are similar, and perhaps it will help encourage and console her."

"Of course," I said. "I believe that God brought us together for such a time as this. Your father told me the same thing."

"Yes, Dad believed that," Tim said. He cocked his head. "There is one thing I don't understand, though. How did you manage not to get the microchips? How did you work and buy goods?"

"About *that*," I said, smiling. "About five years ago, I moved out to the farm in Clare because God had richly blessed me with more than enough. I paid cash for the house, land, and upgrades. God had told me to take money out of the bank every week and convert it to physical gold and silver. That's another reason people close to me thought I was losing my mind. When the federal government forced everyone to get the microchips implanted a few years after the forced vaccine, which I also refused, I was able to buy off the local mayor with some silver. There was indeed a chip registered and a shot given in my name, but neither one is in me—thank God."

Tim looked shocked. "Where is the chip then?"

"Let's say it's out in the wilderness somewhere," I laughed.

Tim laughed along with me. "Let's rest, you righteous rebel," he teased.

As I lay on the ground under the stars cuddling Fire for warmth, I felt tremendous peace come upon me as I drifted into a restful slumber.

*　　*　　*

"Mom, Mom, wake up!" John's voice blared through the walkie that Tim was handing to me. "I want to talk to you!"

I took the walkie. "Hi, John. Good to hear your voice, son, but I asked you not to call us."

"I didn't," he said. "Mr. Tim called us."

"Oh, in that case," I said, "this is the best wake-up call I've had in a while!"

"I miss you, and you've only been gone for a few days. When will you be home, Mom?"

"Well, we are still a long way off. We are fine, though. How is Mike? Have you been prepping for winter?"

"Mr. Mike is pretty much healed. He's been helping us maintain the chicken coop. He developed a way to heat the outdoor trees and vines longer to extend their growing season by using stone walls next to the tree trunks. He also helped us design irrigation ditches so the rainwater will collect and flow to the crops without us needing to lug the water bins to them."

"I'm impressed," I said.

"He's smart," John said. "It is a lot of work! I'm not sure we can do this on our own. The kids can't help much."

"I understand," I told him. "I suggest that you lean on God, pray, and rely on God's grace. Practice listening to God in silence."

"I do." He sighed. "It's still hard."

"I know you can do it. Keep pressing on, son. The battery is running low, and I need to go now. I will contact you when I am able. I love you the mostest," I said, on the verge of tears.

"I love you more than the mostest. Bye."

I handed the walkie back to Tim. "Did you talk to Ruby?"

"Yes. Well, mostly I talked and she listened. She seems to be holding up pretty well."

"I pray for her," I said.

Tim opened the map and pointed to a spot northwest of Clare. "Here's where we are. We're about halfway there. Let's keep moving."

He had already packed up everything, and we started walking north.

"How much food do we have left?" I asked.

"Not much, and no dog food. I fed Fire some dehydrated mashed potatoes, and she likes them!"

"She's not picky," I said. "Should we fish or hunt?"

"No, not yet. It's best to keep moving. I don't like that we saw those two in the car a few days ago. Perhaps we could scavenge a small town.

According to the map, there appears to be one a few miles ahead in this direction."

"Sounds reasonable," I said.

We continued to walk on in silence. The early fall air was cool, and we were thankful it didn't dip below fifty degrees. The sky was overcast and cloudy, but it hadn't rained yet, which was rare for this time of year. We would have to find shelter when the inevitable downpour came.

We walked on for two days, and still the rain did not come. We were critically low on food and had prayed daily for sustenance.

"Hey, stop!" I said, spying a small gas station and convenience store across the road. "Look, left of us. We should check it for food."

Tim hesitated. "I'm not sure it's safe."

I reached out my hand. "Take my hands, and let's pray for guidance." I held Tim's massive strong hands, closed my eyes, and began. "Father God, we see this gas station as an opportunity to find food and water. Please direct us and make it safe for us, in Jesus's name. Amen."

"Amen," Tim echoed.

I motioned for Fire to stay in the woods, and she whined for a bit but ultimately complied. We did an end-around and cautiously approached the small gas station with a convenience store attached. It appeared to be abandoned. Tim crouched down and stood to the side as he opened the front door. The store was dark, and someone had pulled all the signage down, so we didn't even know the name of the place.

Surveying the devastation, Tim said, "Looks like the work of the Fates." He walked outside and inspected the gas pumps but couldn't get the gas flowing.

I walked through aisles of empty shelves, which were dusty and dirty, but found nothing to scavenge. My heart sank. I'd been hoping for some canned food, maybe a few bottles of water—anything. Instead, I found only row upon row of empty shelves. I began to get discouraged.

Check upstairs.

I turned to Tim. "Do you see any doors or a staircase?"

He shook his head and continued walking toward the rear of the store. Suddenly he stopped glanced up at the ceiling. "Look." He pointed to a spot on the ceiling about three feet square that was a bit discolored. "Maybe someone painted over the door to conceal it."

Using a broom handle, he began tapping the ceiling, causing dust to rain down on us. We both coughed. The door finally gave way, and a ladder swung down on its hinges. The rungs of the ladder-stairs creaked under Tim's weight as we slowly ascended into darkness.

I followed him up. I pulled the flashlight out of my backpack and pointed it straight ahead through the dark upper room, which was swirling with dust.

"Food!" Tim exclaimed, pointing to two boxes in the far corner. He ran over and opened the first box. "Sardines." He grimaced. "This is a little better—SpaghettiOs." He smiled and packed the food in his backpack. "Turn around, and I will put the rest in yours."

"Look over there—pop!" My main guilty pleasure, my one weakness, was right in front of me. Wasting no time, I opened a can of Faygo root beer and guzzled it down. I had so missed that sugary sweet taste. I tossed a can to Tim, and he downed it in a single gulp.

"Ah," he said. "Come on; let's go." He walked toward the stairs with a case of Artic Sun Faygo in hand.

We walked back toward the woods where we had left Fire, feeling a bit happier.

Bark, bark! Ruff! Fire greeted us as she began jumping around, running back and forth between us, and wagging her tail as though we had been gone for years instead of minutes.

"Let's walk till nighttime," Tim said lightheartedly, "and then we will feast on our spoils."

"Sounds good." We walked on through the gathering darkness, lost in thought.

Chapter 7
Discoveries

Yet thou in thy manifold mercies forsookest them not in the wilderness: the pillar of the cloud departed not from them by day, to lead them in the way; neither the pillar of fire by night, to shew them light, and the way wherein they should go.

—Nehemiah 9:19 KJV

"I'm tired, and I need to stop and rest," I said, my steps unsteady and my thoughts scattered.

"Are you okay?" Tim asked, taking hold of my arm to steady me.

"I think I forgot to take my thyroid meds for a few days," I said, faltering. The fatigue and mental fog had begun to set in.

"Do you need help?" Tim asked while guiding me to the nearest log in the woods and helping me sit down.

"No," I said, dropping my bag next to me. I rummaged around for a bit before finally finding the bottle of Synthroid I had brought. I took one with some water.

"Are you hungry?" Tim was sitting on the blanket he had spread on the ground next to me.

"No, just tired," I whispered. I watched Tim as he ate cold SpaghettiOs and drinking Faygo Arctic Sun. At one point, he stopped and gave Fire some food and water, which she lapped up happily.

"Okay," he said. "Let me know when you are ready to eat."

"Thank you," I whispered, staring off into the darkness of the woods, listening to the crickets chirping and the owls hooting. It seemed as though hours had passed when I looked back at Tim and saw that he had lain down now with Fire.

He saw me. "Lie down next to me here on this blanket with Fire in the middle. See, Fire likes it!" Tim pointed to a spot next to Fire.

I hesitated. *What does Tim want from me?* I wondered.

He wants to comfort you.

Still, I had feelings for Tim that I had not felt for any man in nearly twenty years.

"Come now," he said, smiling. "Just let me hold you both, nothing more."

"What if the Furies find us?" I replied, still reluctant to lie down next to him.

"Come now. The Furies must sleep sometime; let us sleep, too." Tim had lain down again, hugging Fire close to his body and beckoning me over to lie down next to her.

I conceded eventually. I placed the walkie next to me on the blanket and lay down on my side next to Fire. Tim held us in his arms, providing safety and comfort as I hugged Fire, and we all quickly fell into a deep sleep.

*   *   *

"Wake up, sleepyhead," Tim whispered, gently touching the side of my face.

"I'm up!" I exclaimed, jolting awake in the dim light of dusk.

"Care for some delicious sardines?" Tim offered as he sat next to me on the ground.

"I'd rather have some SpaghettiOs, please?"

"Here you go," Tim said, opening the can and handing it to me.

"Did Fire eat?" I asked after chugging the SpaghettiOs and pop.

"Yep, I gave her water, too," Tim replied while stroking Fire, who was sitting next to him.

I stood up and stretched. "Okay, we should start walking before I fall asleep again." I laughed.

"All right, let's go." Tim led the way.

"So it's your turn," I said. "Tell me something about yourself."

"What do you want to know?"

"Do you remember being adopted?" I asked.

"Not really. Dad showed me pictures of the orphanage and our biological parents, but I have no true memories—just memories of my dad's memories."

I paused for a moment and felt the wind on my face and heard the twigs snapping beneath our feet. "What was it like growing up with Ruth? I mean, how was your relationship?"

"When Ruth and I were younger, we were best friends, and we were in the same classes in school until high school. We studied together, went to Dad's youth group, and played after school. It was nice to have a friend who would never leave you."

"What caused things to change so much in high school?"

"Well, Dad moved his church out this way right before we started high school. We didn't know anyone at the new school, and we were different from everyone else there."

"Different how?" I asked.

"We had better tans," he said with a laugh.

I laughed with him. "I see."

"Yeah, not many kids looked like us, and the ones who did had black parents, not white parents like ours. It was obvious that we were adopted. Ruth had it a bit rougher than I did, and she struggled in school and was placed in remedial classes while I attended the advanced-placement classes. The kids made fun of her long, skinny legs and long, straight black hair."

"Kids are so cruel," I said, recalling my own high school experience. "I bet Ruth looked beautiful."

"She really did. The kids were jealous. I got teased occasionally too, but I didn't let it bother me too much. I had Opal, my future wife, so it was different for me."

"How were things at home?"

"Great for me. My parents were happy I was on track for a college scholarship. They liked Opal and her family, and I never complained about anything. I helped my dad with chores, looked after the animals after school, and willingly attended youth group and Sunday services. My mom was sick a lot, so I had to help her with household chores and cooking, too."

"Yes, your dad told me your mom died of cancer. I'm so sorry."

"Thank you, Lilly," Tim said. "It was such a long time ago. Ruth didn't take Mom's death well at all. She got more despondent, clinging to Ash and pulling away from us."

"You never liked Ash? Why?"

"Well, I'm not sure. There was just something about him. His demeanor was off. I was probably the only one who saw Ash's true self at school. I begged Ruth not to marry him, but she wouldn't listen. I prayed for them both. I still do," he whispered.

"Now for a fun question," I said, sensing the need to lighten the mood.

"Oh happy day!" he said.

"What's your favorite color?"

"Green," he said. "Hunter green, like the pine trees in summer. How about you?"

"Midnight blue," I said. "What's your favorite food?"

"Cold SpaghettiOs fresh from the can and Artic Sun," he said. "Oh, and with a side of sardines."

We both laughed.

"Seriously," Tim said, "it was definitely my mother's homemade lasagna and garlic bread with black forest cake for dessert." Tim paused, as if remembering happier, simpler times, then asked, "And you?"

"Jet's deep-dish square cheese pizza with ranch dressing. Yum, now I'm craving pizza!"

"Father God, please bring us pizza!" Tim said, laughing.

"Amen! That would be amazing." I sighed.

We walked on in silence for the remainder of the night. As the sun rose, I said, "We should find a place to sleep soon."

"I agree. Let's walk closer to the road," Tim said, "and maybe we can find a vacant cabin or house."

"Sounds good," I replied, following him toward the edge of the woods on the side of a small county road.

"Stop. Look." Tim pointed off to the left. "There's a tiny house set back a bit from the road."

I laughed. "I don't see anything!"

"Come on. Follow me and be quiet," Tim instructed.

I followed him in the dim early-morning daylight.

After turning onto a narrow dirt road to the right, we ended up at a small trailer home with mold growing on the outside, covering the white siding. Overgrown grass and trees threatened to overtake the house itself.

"It looks empty." Tim waved me on. "Come."

"Ew, it smells horrible here!" I exclaimed, sidestepping trash and animal feces.

"Yeah," he said. "This place has seen better days. Let's try the bedroom in the back."

I wedged a chair under the front door, and Fire and I followed Tim to the only bedroom in the house. The small room had a queen-size bed, a decaying brown dresser, and many cobwebs. It did smell a bit better, though.

"I'm exhausted," I said, plopping down on the bed and letting my backpack drop onto the floor.

"You don't want to eat?" Tim asked.

"No, I just want to sleep," I replied groggily.

"All right," he said. "Don't forget to take your meds. I'll sleep in the chair in the living room. Give a shout if you need me." Tim shut the door behind him with Fire at his heels.

Finally alone, I drifted off into a deep sleep.

"Mom, wake up!" John shouted at me through the walkie Tim was holding next to my ear.

"I'm up," I coughed.

"Are you okay, Mom?" John asked, concerned.

"Yes, just a lot of dust in this bed. What have you been up to?"

"We've been starting to harvest berries, apples, pears, and plums. The girls have been canning them. This morning we went hunting and got another deer. I just finished smoking it."

"You don't know how delicious that sounds about now," I told him. "How is Mike doing?"

"He's doing okay. He was able to help a little bit with the harvesting. He just went to bed."

"Well, you take care," I said. "It sounds like you're doing a great job, and I'm very proud of you, son. We need to get moving now, so I'll let you go. Love you most."

"Love you the mostest, Mom. Bye."

"Come on into the kitchen," Tim said, leading the way out of the bedroom. "I have a treat! I found some cinnamon oatmeal."

I washed the oatmeal down with water and was happy that the putrid smell was overpowered by the smell of fresh cinnamon oatmeal.

It was time to go. We headed out into the cool, dark night with our night-vision goggles on.

Some hours later, Tim stopped abruptly, held up his hand, and whispered, "Shush! There are people up ahead."

I blew the whistle and motioned for Fire to be quiet and lie down.

"I see them now," I said. "Should we move closer?"

"Yes," Tim replied while slowly creeping toward the little camping tent, careful to stay hidden in the trees.

We carefully surveyed the small campsite. Sleeping around a dead fire were a man, a woman, and a small child. They didn't seem to have any gear other than a small tent encircled by tin cans and zipped up tight. I scanned the woods surrounding us as best I could in the night. We were the only ones out tonight. An owl hooted in the distance as we watched the sleeping family.

"Should we wake them?" I whispered.

"No, let's watch for a bit and see if they wake up. The family seems friendly, and I want to see if they have seen the Furies here lately."

"I'm not sure they're friendly," I said. "I hope they are, but what if they are decoys working for the Furies, like James from the pharmacy in the town where your father lived?"

"Let's pray," Tim said. He took my hand. "Father God, tell us what to do. In Jesus's name. Amen."

"Amen," I whispered.

A still, small voice answered: "Wait."

"Wait it is," Tim replied as he sat down in the brush beside their campsite.

"Okay," I said as I sat down next to Tim.

*   *   *

"Awake, child."

I jolted awake and saw a friendly older woman with long gray hair, pale wrinkly skin, and blue eyes standing over me. "Who are you? Where is Tim?" I demanded, reaching for my gun.

"He's over at camp with my daughter and her family," the woman said. "We won't hurt you," she assured me.

"Lilly, you're awake." Tim smiled and waved me over to him. "Come on over here. It's safe."

I let the old lady lead the way back to camp as I scanned the woods for Fire, not noticing that she was sitting next to Tim. "How long have I been asleep?" I asked.

"Long enough," Tim said. "Let me introduce you to the Cohens. This young lady is Jenny; David is her husband; and the little one, their daughter, is Rachel. Oh, and their mother's name is Mary, whom you've already met."

"Hello, everyone," I replied, shaking hands and sitting next to Tim.

"Lilly, they're on their way to the Upper Peninsula!" Tim exclaimed. "Can you believe that?"

"What! Why?" I asked, surprised.

David answered. "We have a small off-grid cabin near Kinross. I thought it would be safe there, away from the Furies, especially with my mother-in-law the way she is."

"What's wrong with Mary?" I asked. "She seems fine to me."

"My mother has advanced dementia," Jennifer explained with a hint of sadness in her voice. "And she won't remember you when you leave."

"Rachel, come back here!" David yelled as the small child began to stray too far into the woods.

"How old is Rachel?" I asked.

"Five," Jennifer answered.

"I love that age. They are so innocent." I admired Rachel's curly red hair, pale skin, and green eyes; she was a miniature replica of her mother and father.

"Yes. Sadly innocence is not such a good thing nowadays," David said.

"It could be," Tim advised wisely. "You just have to guide Rachel and watch her closely."

"Yes, we are," Jennifer responded as Rachel climbed into her lap, hugging her mother shyly and avoiding contact with us.

"Good," Tim said. "Have you seen the Furies out this way?"

David answered. "Last week we saw two of them driving south, and we haven't seen any since."

"A man and a woman?" Tim asked. "Maybe a cigar-smoking woman?"

"Yes," David replied. "I take it you saw them too. Want some fish? I caught it this morning."

"Yes, thanks!" Tim said.

"No, thank you," I said.

David doled out portions of fish to the others.

Silence fell as everyone ate, including Fire, and I watched them. *Friendly people*, I thought. *But I still don't trust them.*

You can trust them. It is okay.

"What are you thinking about, Lilly?" Tim asked as he tossed some fish bones into the fire.

"That we should get moving soon," I answered.

"Where are you all headed?" David asked between bites.

"We are heading northwest," Tim answered, careful not to divulge the exact location.

"Why out there?" Jennifer asked.

"I have family out that way," Tim said. "I want to see if they made it."

"Yes, the rest of my family initially got taken by the Furies," David stated sadly. "We barely made it out of Grand Rapids on day one." David fell silent.

"I just don't understand why the Fates are doing this!" Jennifer exclaimed, exasperated.

"Power, money, evil," I answered. "Take your pick."

She didn't answer.

"We should go, Tim," I said.

"Yes, I agree. Good-bye, friends. May God bless you on your travels," Tim said as he shook their hands.

"Bye," I said, waving as we walked away, the heady autumn smell of woodsmoke in my nostrils.

Some hours later, Tim said, "What did you think of David and Jennifer?"

"I prayed, and the Holy Spirit said they were okay. Therefore, I trust them for now unless they prove me wrong."

"They're okay," Tim said. "I hope they make it to the Upper Peninsula before winter."

"Yes, and I hope we find Ruth before winter too," I added.

"We will have faith," Tim assured.

"Is it almost night again? I slept that long?" I squinted while stumbling on some branches in the dim light.

"Yes, you slept a long time," Tim said. He turned and looked at me, concerned. "Are you feeling okay, Lilly?"

"Yes, it's just all the walking and the thyroid—lack of a thyroid," I said. "I get exhausted a lot."

Tim smiled. "We need to pray for more coffee!"

"Yes, God, please bring us more coffee. In Jesus's name, I pray. Amen."

"Yes, amen!" Tim exclaimed.

Some hours later, in the dark of night, I slowed and said, "I need to take a break. I can't walk any farther right now."

"Well, look over there, under the pines. We can rest there for a while." Tim pointed into the darkness.

"You lead," I answered groggily.

"Here you go. Lie down on my backpack," Tim instructed. He helped me down to the ground.

I laid my head upon his backpack, which was propped against a log, and yawned. "We should call the kids again."

"It's late," Tim said. "I doubt they will be awake. Let's pray for Mike, the kids, and our new friends. Father God, protect our new friends on their way to the Upper Peninsula. Protect the kids back home and give them wisdom and peace. Continue to guide us to Ruth, and watch over us in the night. In Jesus's name we pray. Amen"

"Amen," I said. "Aren't you going to sleep, Tim?"

"No, you go ahead," he said. "I'm going to stay awake a while. Good night, Lilly."

"Good night, Tim," I said, and I then quickly fell into a deep sleep.

Chapter 8
The Hiding Place

Have not I commanded thee? Be strong and of a good
courage; be not afraid, neither be thou dismayed: for the
Lord thy God is with thee whithersoever thou goest.

—Joshua 1:9 KJV

"Get up already!" the deep voice yelled while kicking me.
"Ow! Tim, stop!" I commanded," struggling to open my eyes.

"It's not me, Lilly," Tim said. "Please do as they say."

I jolted awake then to find Tim handcuffed on his knees, his eyes
swollen and his nose bloodied. A younger man who appeared to be
following the older and meaner man was holding Tim down. The older
man was the one kicking and yelling at me.

"Shut up," he growled as he turned and struck Tim again.

I got up quickly and looked around. I couldn't see Fire anywhere and
hoped she was okay.

What should I do? I prayed in my head.

*Fire is hiding in the woods, and I commanded her to follow at a distance.
Be patient, do as they say, and I will provide a way out.*

I took a deep breath and waited for the mean old man to tell me
what to do. I trembled in fear as he bound my hands in chains. I saw the
walkie, hidden in a nearby bush, still in perfect condition. They had our
backpacks, but they didn't have the walkie.

Please don't let John call, I prayed.

The younger man held a gun to the back of Tim's head, towering over him with big, bulging muscles, while the older, shorter man yanked the chains and moved me forward. He snarled, "Start walking; don't stop or you're both dead."

He pulled us south off the trail we had been following and farther into the woods. I stumbled often on the thick roots and other foliage as he dragged me forward. We arrived at a dirt road, crossed it, and walked on for about ten minutes. I glanced over at Tim, and my heart sank. He had been beaten savagely. Blood was streaming from the cuts on his face and arms, and his left eye was swollen beyond recognition. He looked down as he trudged along. We came to a stop in front of an abandoned old building. Somebody had boarded up the windows, and the lights were out. A sign on the front read "Ed's Garage."

"Let us in!" the older man demanded as he banged on the makeshift wooden door. I suspected the glass door had been torn down.

"Who's there?" a gruff man's voice responded.

"Jake and Dominic, you idiot!" the older man dragging me said. "Open up now! Hurry up! We have them," the elder man shouted, becoming angrier by the second.

"Sorry, Dominic," the man said as he opened the door. Dominic yanked our chains, forcing us inside as the heavyset man promptly shut the door behind us.

"You're a dang moron, Jim," Dominic chided while yanking us down several hallways.

Jim shuffled along behind us, head down, unspeaking, accepting his low station in life—a failure even among other morons. The hallway was long and dark and smelled of mold and motor oil. It looked like a dungeon, but it was not. We stopped at the door on my right, which was probably the former manager's office—maybe the owner Ed's office. A small window overlooked the garage bays to enable the manager to supervise the mechanics' work. One older car sat on a lift high in the air. Tools and thick black grease covered the floor. Someone was hung by their hands from a chain in the far corner of the garage.

"Here," Dominic growled as he shoved me inside. I turned and shouted frantically, "What are you doing with Tim?"

He shoved me hard onto the cement floor. "That's none of your business," he snarled, spitting saliva with every word, sweat dripping from his slightly wrinkled forehead. He turned to Jake and said, "Watch her, and make sure she doesn't escape."

Jake nodded and closed the door as Dominic began dragging Tim to another part of the garage.

Jake stood guard outside with his back to the door. He didn't speak, leaving me to wonder what would happen next. I was thankful they didn't know my name. I surveyed the dimly lit room. I stood up slowly, chains shaking, noticing my tailbone was sore from Dominic's shoving me to the ground.

Even though Dominic appeared to be in his early fifties, he stood about six feet two and had the strength of a twenty-year-old. His eyes were dark and his soul vacant. I shuddered, praying Tim would be okay.

There was a bowl of water on a chair beneath a smaller metal desk in the middle of the room. The small, white-walled room was a stark contrast to the dark and dingy hallway. It was obviously an office. A floor lamp standing in the far right corner behind the desk cast shadows on the wall. The room was clean, unlike the rest of the rooms I had seen.

The metal office chair hurt my tailbone, so I opted to stand in the corner and wait (for what, I did not know). I couldn't hear much, just the sound of a heavy door slamming somewhere off in the distance.

The silence made me anxious, and I feared what would come next. "Holy Spirit, comfort me," I whispered. Immediately the fear dissipated, replaced by hope.

Check the desk.

I tiptoed quietly over to the desk, to minimize the sound of my chains rattling, careful not to alert Jake. I very carefully opened the long, thin drawer, the only one with a handle.

Screech.

I stopped and looked up at Jake, whose back was still to the door. Apparently he hadn't heard a thing. The drawer wouldn't open fully, so I gathered up the long chains that bound me in my left hand and yanked harder with my right, which caused the metal desk to shake. Again Jake ignored me or didn't hear. I continued trying to wiggle the drawer open.

Snap. The desk drawer had opened, and it appeared there was nothing inside the actual drawer. I closed it halfway and reached my left hand into the space where the end of the drawer met the back of the desk.

"Ow," I whispered as the drawer pinched my arm when I reached back as far as I could. I felt a piece of plastic wedged in the tiny space where the drawer met the desk. I began to wiggle it out along with my hand. I put the small plastic box in my pocket.

"What's going on in there?" Jake screamed angrily while opening the door and scanning his eyes around the room.

I quickly shut the drawer and sat down on the floor in the corner across from the lamp, not responding or making eye contact with him.

"Shut up and stay put," Jake ordered while slamming the door behind him. "*Or else!*"

"Phew, that was close," I whispered.

I noticed that the lamp was casting a shadow across my side of the room and that the temperature inside had dropped. Jake's tall, thin frame didn't frighten me; nor did his jade-green eyes and olive skin. It was Dominic whose vacant, soulless black eyes sent shivers down my spine. I sat down and covered myself with the green blanket on the floor next to me, leaned against the wall, closed my eyes, and let time pass.

I awoke in deep darkness to the loud clank of a metal door slamming, followed by several deep-throated screams. I crawled quietly toward the door, cracked it slightly. I couldn't see anything but darkness—no Jake, no anything. I angled the lamp toward the window, careful not to alert the Furies.

A horrific sight assaulted my eyes. Two figures hung from the ceiling by chains, their feet dangling just above the cold concrete floor. The men paused briefly every so often before continuing their savage beating of the captives.

"Oh no, Tim!" I cried, tears streaming down my face. "Father God, please help! Protect Tim and whoever is with him. Show us the way out," I prayed quietly.

Wait and do not fear.

"I rebuke you, spirit of fear!" I quietly exclaimed. "Father God, please send your angel armies to fight for us. In Jesus's name I pray. Amen." I finished and fell silent, feeling at once hyped up and drained. I needed my thyroid meds.

As I sat on the tattered green blanket on the cold concrete floor, it took everything in me to stay positive and go on. At least the Furies hadn't gotten the walkie, though we had no way to contact home. *We could go back for it*, I thought. *But what now?* Being bound in chains again was so frustrating. I had been free for twenty years and now was in physical chains again.

The song "Fear Is a Liar" by Zach Williams kept playing over and over in my head.

"Ah yes, thank You, Holy Spirit, for reminding me, when things seem bad, to make a joyful noise," I quietly exclaimed, and I began singing the song over and over in a whisper.

"Be quiet!" Jake threw open the door, stomped over to me, slapped me across the face hard, then yelled, "I'm not gonna tell you again!"

"Ow," I whispered, rubbing my left cheek as he stomped out again, slamming the door behind him.

My stomach growled, and I regretted my decision not to eat some of the fish David had offered. I was confused and not sure how many days we had been there, because the closed garage bay doors let no sunlight pass inside.

Ah! I remembered that I had been prompted to take some of my thyroid pills out of the bottle in my backpack and carry them in my pockets. Now I knew why. *Thank You, Lord!*

I stuffed my hands deep into my pockets and searched frantically for my medicine. I choked down some pills without water. "Thank You, Jesus, for not letting them find these pills!"

I slipped into a deep sleep.

*   *   *

"Wake up!" Dominic shouted, shaking my shoulders harshly but at least not kicking me this time. "We have some questions!"

"I'm up," I replied, squinting at the fluorescent flashlight Jake was shining directly in my face.

"Now, answer my questions or you'll get this!" Dominic cracked a jagged leather whip close enough to my face to make me cringe.

"Ha, ha!" Jake jeered at me. "She's scared."

"Shut up, you idiot!" Dominic shouted. "And I told you to change the bulbs in this flashlight!" Dominic snatched the flashlight out of Jake's hand and smashed the lens against the desk.

"I forgot." Jake sulked as he turned on the desk lamp.

"What's your name, girl!" Dominic shouted.

"Li-Li-Lilly," I stuttered, staring at the floor upon which I sat.

"Well, Li-Li-Lilly, why are you traveling with Tim?"

"I met him a few weeks ago," I replied, still avoiding eye contact. "Why?"

Dominic paused and then asked in a menacing tone, "Are you one of Ruth's friends?"

"No, I don't know a Ruth. Who is she to you?"

"I ask the questions!" Dominic ordered, cracking the whip against the front of my legs.

"Ah!" I screamed, as my cargo pants offered little protection.

"I'll ask again," he said, lowering his voice. "Do you know where Ruth is?"

"I don't know Ruth or where she is! But even if I did, I wouldn't tell you!" I yelled back at him, glaring defiantly.

"Tell me why you're with Tim!" Dominic shouted again, inches from my face.

"I already told you!" I shouted back. "I met him in the woods! We were hiding from you!"

"Shut up!" Jake yelled. He then turned to Dominic. "Want me to take care of her for you?"

"No, moron," Dominic replied, laughing. "Ash wants her brought in alive."

"Are you the girl who was down at the pharmacy a few weeks ago with dogs and gold?" Dominic asked.

"Do you see a dog, or gold in my bag?" I asked.

"I ask the questions, little girl!" Dominic slammed his fist on the desk.

So they think I'm a young girl, I thought. *Not too bright. Thank You, Lord, for my baby face ... and their stupidity.*

"Aren't you too young for Tim?" Dominic teased.

"I told you we're just friends," I said calmly. "I met him a few weeks ago in the woods."

Dominic glared at me, seemingly wanting to ask another question, but then he suddenly got up, commanding, "Come on, Jake; we'll get it out of Tim!"

"See *you* later," Jake said with a wink, slamming the door behind them.

"Finally," I whispered. I inspected the stripes spanning across the front of both of my thighs.

"Ah!" a man's voice screamed in torment, followed by silence.

I walked slowly to the window and peeked out and saw Tim and the other man, heads hung down, not moving or speaking.

"We need to go tell Ash!" Jake screamed.

"Enough! I am in charge," Dominic said. He punched Jake in the face. "You answer to me! I need to figure this out!"

With blood pouring from his nose and over his mouth, Jake said, "You're wasting time. Asha is getting away!"

"What about these three?" Dominic mused as he paced the hallway. "They'll slow us down."

"I'll watch them," Jim stammered nervously, avoiding contact as he stood behind them in the shadows.

"You sure you won't kill them like last time?" Dominic asked.

"I was having a bad day," Jim replied. "What do you want me to do with them?"

"Whatever you want," Dominic said. "Just don't kill them, whether you're having a bad day or not. Or I'll kill you. Got it? Try to get the little girl to tell the truth."

Jim nodded and looked toward my room with a lurid smile that sent shivers down my spine. I shrank back into the corner and sat down on the blanket.

I heard the ominous sound of feet stomping down the hallway, and then the front door banging. My hands trembled as Jim's loud footfalls grew louder until he was just outside the door.

"God help us," I prayed repeatedly.

"*Huh, huh.*" I heard panting as the door slowly opened.

"Fire," I whispered. She came upon me stealthily, licking my wounds and nuzzling me with her face. I could barely make out her tail wagging in the darkness.

I heard footsteps shuffling toward me as Fire turned and looked at the door. Her shepherd stripe stood straight up along the whole length of her back as she let out a deep, throaty growl that was barely audible. I pulled the dog whistle out from under my jacket and blew it, commanding her to hush. I pointed toward the dark corner to the right of the door. She immediately went there and lay down, hiding, waiting.

The door slammed. "Where are you?" Jim asked as he entered the room. He had a lit candle in one hand and a bloody belt in another.

I froze in terror, knowing it had to be Tim's blood. I sat in the corner, both arms clenched around my legs, chains dangling, not wanting to make eye contact with the evil man.

"We're going to play a game," Jim said as he set the candle on the desk and began shuffling toward me. He smelled foul, like cigarettes and beer. He was wearing a stained white T-shirt and tattered dirty jeans two sizes too big for him. He had a long crimson scar that ran from his left eye down to his chin, and several star-shaped tattoos covering his neck and arms. His greasy black hair and penetrating brown eyes repulsed me, and he seemed to sense my thoughts.

"Now that we're alone," he said, sneering, "you will tell me your real name!"

I sat there silent, looking at the ground, afraid to move.

Crack! His belt snapped down beside me, causing me to jump.

"Scared you, huh?" He laughed. "It would be a shame to mess up your pretty little-girl face," he whispered, pushing back my long blonde hair and kneeling next to me. He ripped open my shirt and squeezed my breasts hard.

"Stop, that hurts!" I screamed.

"No."

Tears wetted my cheeks, and I was falling back twenty years.

"What are you going to do about it?" He laughed as he shifted his body over me, bracing himself with one hand against the wall behind me, holding me down with the other, his putrid breath causing me to vomit in my mouth.

I pushed at him, hitting him. "Help!" I screamed. He paused for a moment.

"No one is coming," he said, letting go of me so he could rear up and smack me hard across the face. He raised his hand to strike me again, and I winced and turned my head to shield my face from the blow.

"What the—?" he shouted. "Something bit me." He screamed, rolled over, and scanned the room.

Fire pounced again from behind, sinking her teeth into his neck. Jim stood up, stumbling and falling into the furniture, blood pouring from the wound.

"Who's the tough guy now?!" I screamed, wrapping the chain around his neck and choking the life out of him. I stood shaking over his lifeless body, crying. I grabbed the keys that hung from his belt and unlocked the chains that bound my hands.

"Fire, come here, girl!" She stopped licking the blood off her fur and immediately came to my side, and I petted her. "Good girl," I said. "Come; let's find Tim."

I didn't see them hanging out there in the garage anymore. "Fire, go find Tim, girl!"

Fire ran down the hallway, stopping to pick up his scent along the way. We did seem to be alone now. Apparently Dominic had thought Jim could handle things by himself.

We had to hurry. I hoped we could get far away from here before the other two returned. I shuddered to think what condition Tim would be in when we found him.

Fire stopped near a closed metal door, pawing at it, trying to get in. I blew the dog whistle and motioned for her to stop and wait behind me. I opened the large metal door and saw Tim lying in the corner beside a badly injured man tied to a metal rack. A wooden workbench with bloody tools on it stood next to them.

"Tim, wake up!" I exclaimed.

"Lilly," he whispered. "Am I dreaming? How did you escape?"

"God sent Fire to help," I answered, frantically pulling at his chains and unlocking them with Jim's keys.

"Good dog," he said, his eyes struggling to focus.

"Stay with me, Tim," I said. "We have to get out of here before Dominic gets back. Can you stand?"

"I think so." Tim struggled to form the words, but once I had freed him, he pulled himself up and leaned against the workbench for support. Tim limped slowly toward the door, dragging his right leg behind him. "Here," he said, tossing our backpacks to me. "You'll have to carry both bags."

"What about him?" I asked, nodding toward the other man, who was cowering in the corner.

"Leave him," Tim said. "He's a traitor, and he's the one who sent the Furies out to get you. He's from the pharmacy. He betrayed you." He groaned.

"James?" I said, hardly recognizing his bloody, beaten face.

"I'm sorry," he said, "but they were going to kill my family. They thought you had more gold." He choked on the blood and tears streaming down his face.

"Did you tell them who I am?" I demanded.

"No," he said, "and they forgot to check your backpacks, too."

"Where are they going?" I asked.

"West, to find Asha," James said. "There's a microchip scanner and deactivator in that drawer. Please take it. Leave me. They will come back and kill us all." James slowly lifted his arm and pointed at the large metal drawer under the workbench.

"Why are you helping us?" I asked.

"My wife and children are hiding in the woods. Please help them," James pleaded.

"Lilly, come on," Tim said. "We need to leave now." Adrenaline was flowing, and he was sounding stronger, more urgent, as he beckoned me out the door. He had picked up the scanner and put it in his pocket but then fell into the door as he turned to leave, and he nearly went down.

"Tim!" I rushed to grab him, but his weight was too much for me to bear.

"Here," I said, "take this broom and use it as a crutch."

"That's better," he replied. "Let's go." Somehow he managed to smile at me through the pain.

"Wait," I said. "Let me take a quick look through the rest of the cabinets. Awesome! First-aid supplies, dehydrated food, and bottled water!" I threw everything into my bag.

We strode out into the cold night, Fire running ahead of us, thankful that the moon was shining upon us, lighting our way. We stopped frequently, as Tim had a hard time hobbling along.

"You should just leave me and get as far away as possible," Tim pleaded.

"Like that's going to happen," I said. "No, I won't leave you. Hush with that nonsense."

We walked north into the woods, Tim hobbling beside me.

"We need to get a good distance away and then find somewhere to hide tonight," I said as we walked deeper into the woods and into the dark.

Several hours later, Tim stopped. "I need to find a place to rest. I can't go on much longer."

"Okay," I said. "I see a dirt road up ahead. Let's follow it."

"All right," Tim answered weakly.

We came to a small vacant log cabin just off the dirt road in the woods. Tim followed slowly behind me on one side, and Fire on the other.

"Here, take my hand," I said as we climbed the stairs onto the front porch.

Tim took my hand and made it up the steps with the help of the broom, moaning and groaning all the way.

"Almost there; you've got this," I said.

"Whew!" Tim exclaimed as he fell onto a small couch in the one-room cabin.

"I knew you could do it!" I said while lighting a candle from my bag and wedging a wooden chair against the door.

"This is a nice little place," Tim said. He sipped the water I had brought him.

"Yes, the little wooden table and three tiny cots remind me of 'Goldilocks and the Three Bears'!" I laughed as I at last collapsed onto a wooden chair.

"My mom used to read me that story too!" Tim coughed.

"All right, that's enough excitement for you. Let me see your wounds." I took some alcohol swabs from the first-aid kit.

"Ouch," he said, wincing. "That stings." I cleaned the blood from his face and leg.

"Your foot looks broken," I said, "but you're the doc."

"Animal doc," he said, trying to smile. "I think it's just a bad ankle sprain. I didn't hear any bones break."

"Here, take this aspirin," I said, handing him two pills and a water bottle.

"Thank you for saving me," he said.

"That was all the Good Lord's doing, with the assistance of Fire!"

"Thank God and Fire," he said. "I need to sleep now." Tim closed his eyes and quickly nodded off.

My stomach ached with gnawing hunger pangs, as I hadn't eaten in many days. And unless she had caught some food in the wilds, Fire hadn't eaten in a while either. "You deserve the best dinner I can give you, life-saver," I whispered, thinking, *She might have literally saved our lives.* "Want dinner?"

"Urh?" Fire whined excitedly, wiggling her entire body.

"Okay, shhh," I commanded as I dumped a package of dehydrated potatoes I found in the cupboard into a tin bowl and placed it on the floor next to her along with a dish of water.

"Thank you, God, for this food, water, and shelter!" I exclaimed before digging in to the last can of SpaghettiOs.

By the light of the candle, I could see one small window toward the back of the cabin, a simple black wood-burning stove, and a small freezer standing next to the sink. The log cabin had wood floors and walls covered in dust and thick cobwebs.

After eating, I blew out the candle and lay down on the cot with Fire at my side to warm me and fell into a deep sleep.

"Lilly, help," Tim called.

"I'm up!" I jumped off the cot, the sun shining in my eyes, blocking my view of Tim.

"Come here, please," Tim said, holding out his hand.

"I'm coming," I called to him, fetching the first-aid kit.

"Help me to the table," he said, smiling weakly. "I'm a bit stiff."

I handed him the broom handle and stood under his left arm as he pulled himself up, using me to steady himself. "Let's hurry," I said, straining as we staggered slowly toward the table. "I can't hold you up for long."

"Thank you," Tim said after dropping into the wooden chair.

"How are you?" I asked.

"I'm still in pain, but not as bad as last night." Tim smiled. "I feel weak. Do we have anything to eat?"

"Let me see," I said, and I rummaged through the small metal cupboards.

"Nice!" I said. "God answered our prayers."

"More yummy sardines?" Tim laughed.

"Nice to see your sense of humor is back," I said. "Coffee and oatmeal!" I brought the goods to the table.

"Awesome! God is so good," Tim said. He added Folgers instant coffee to his mug of water and dug into the oatmeal.

After we ate and I took my meds, I looked at Tim and asked, "Are you strong enough to walk a few miles today?"

He shook his head. "No, I need to rest one more day."

I helped him hobble back to the couch. "Here, take these." I handed him two aspirin tablets and a glass of water.

"Thank you," he said. "It is nice resting here in the cabin, Lilly." He smiled. "But we will have to pick up our pace tomorrow, because—"

"Ruth," I finished.

"Yes, we must find her."

"Wait," I said. I went in and got the ice pack I had seen in the back of the freezer. "This will help." I placed it on Tim's ankle.

"That feels much better," he said. "I will rest easy now!" He closed his eyes.

"Me, too," I whispered. I lay back down on the cot and dropped into a restful sleep.

*   *   *

"Lilly, wake up," Tim called. "Look what I found!"

I opened my eyes to find him standing on one leg, leaning against the sink. "How did you get back over to the sink?"

"Fire helped me. My ankle is feeling much better. See, the swelling has gone down" He raised his leg toward me.

"Awesome," I said, sitting up on the cot. "Praise God for healing."

"Amen to that!" Tim sat down in the kitchen chair. "Look," he said, pointing to the open cabinet below the sink.

I squinted as my eyes adjusted to the light and saw more freeze-dried coffee, canned peaches, canned beans, dog food, and more. "Thank You, Jesus!" I exclaimed.

"Yes, thank You, God, for this delicious food."

After the three of us consumed our fill of the food and coffee, I turned to Tim. "Are you able to travel now?"

"Yes." He nodded, lifted his foot off the floor, and rotated it. "I think I can travel slowly. You'll still have to carry the backpacks, though, at first."

"Of course," I said. "Do you think we should go back for the walkie? What if the Fates find it?"

"No," he said, shaking his head. "I think we should keep moving ahead."

"All right," I agreed. "We need to find Ruth. Let's continue to the lavender farm." I stood up and gathered both backpacks.

Tim hobbled out the door with the help of the broom handle.

"How much farther do you suppose we have to go, Tim?"

"According to the map I was studying this morning, we are halfway there."

"Let's hope the last half will be easier," I said.

"Amen to that," he agreed.

The going was slow, but we managed to walk many hours through the frosty darkness. I shivered. "Brr, it's cold tonight."

"Yes, summer is long gone now," Tim replied.

"I see another small cabin up ahead that looks abandoned." I adjusted my night-vision goggles. "Want to stop for the rest of the night and get warm?"

"I thought you'd never ask," he said, sighing. "I could use a break."

"No steps this time," I noted as we neared the cabin.

"Great," Tim replied. He pushed open the white metal door and hobbled inside.

"At least this one is clean," I said, glancing around the one-bedroom cabin, which was only marginally dusty.

"Looks like someone cleaned it before they left, and the lock on this front door still works." Tim shut the door behind us and locked it.

"It's cozy," I said. I dropped the backpacks on the floor and collapsed on the soft green loveseat.

"Yes," Tim said. He leaned back in the black recliner. "This recliner is almost better than your red recliner at home."

"I'm too tired to eat," I said. "I'm going to rest a bit."

"Me too," Tim said, closing his eyes.

* * *

"Lilly, wake up!" Tim called from the kitchen several hours later.

"Ugh, do I have to?" I yawned, struggling to open my eyes.

"Only if you want breakfast," Tim replied as he sat down at the table.

"And what's on the menu this morning?" I walked over to the table.

"Gourmet delight!" Tim said. "Cornflakes, coffee, and water."

"You seem to be getting around a lot better," I noted.

"The swelling is down, and I can bear some weight on it now."

"Where's Fire? Did you feed her, too?"

He nodded. "Yes, I gave her the rest of the dog food and let her out a few hours ago."

"Well, she might not be back for a while," I said.

"That's fine," he replied. "The sun's still up, and I'd rather travel at night." He narrowed his eyes. "What's wrong with your leg?" Tim motioned toward a trickle of blood running down my left calf.

I blotted the blood with a cloth. "The Furies whipped me with a leather belt when I wouldn't tell them where Ruth is. They thought I was lying." I began to clean and rebandage the wounds.

"I have a better idea," Tim said. "Hand me the first-aid kit."

"Use this liquid bandage under the gauze," Tim instructed. "It will be like stitches without a needle."

"Ow, that stings!" I winced as I painted the liquid on my wounds and wrapped them up again.

"Come sit and talk with me," Tim said as he hobbled back over to the couch.

"About what?" I asked, sitting next to him.

Smiling, Tim said, "Did you ever think we would see each other again after leaving the Spring Hill camp all those years ago?"

"No, not really. I had hoped we would keep in touch, but we were so young, and we had no internet!" I laughed.

"Yeah, it's been so easy these last twenty years to find anyone, connect with anyone; and now, in the so-called new world order, we've gone backward." He shook his head and shrugged.

"I pray someday we will be free from the Fates," I said, "so our civilization can start over."

Tim shook his head. "I'm thinking that this is the beginning of the end, Lilly … that Jesus is coming soon."

"Maybe," I said. "But what would change, though? I know I'm going to heaven when our Lord and Savior comes back, and I would rather do God's work here and spend time with friends and family instead of focusing on the end."

"That is a good way to look at things," Tim said.

The room fell silent then for several minutes until we heard *"Erh, erh,"* as Fire whined while scratching the front door.

"I'll let her in," I said, and I went to the door. "No way! Good girl!" I exclaimed as Fire pushed me aside and ran over and dropped the walkie in Tim's hands.

"What!" Tim exclaimed in awe. "Prayers answered!"

"Thank you, Jesus," I said as I petted Fire and gave her some much-deserved food and water.

Tim turned on the walkie and said, "Hello, anyone there?"

After a pause, Mike responded. "Hi, Tim, we were wondering when you would call. How are you two doing?"

"Are the kids around?" Tim asked, hesitant to talk about our circumstances in front of them.

"No, they're out hunting and gathering," Mike replied. "The harvest is bountiful, and God has richly blessed us this season."

"In that case, we had a run-in with the Furies. We escaped a few days ago, and I've got some bruises and a sprained ankle, and Lilly has a few wounds."

"But you two are going to be okay?" Mike asked, sounding concerned.

"Sure," Tim said. "We'll be fine. Just pray for us."

"And please don't tell the kids!" I shouted into the walkie. "No need to worry them."

Tim raised his eyebrows at me and began talking again. "Yes, what she said. We lost a lot of time, and we might not make it home for winter."

"That's too bad," Mike said. "We had hoped you would make it back sooner. We had another refugee arrive the other day. Her name is Emily."

"Is she by herself?" I asked.

"Yes, she's only about twenty-one—a tall, thin young woman with green eyes and blonde hair. She escaped a Fury outpost in Detroit, but the Furies killed her mom and dad. She's fitting right in. In fact, she's out with the girls right now tending to the crops and gathering fruit."

"That's great to hear," Tim said. "Soon we will have no room left in the house."

"Well, we moved the beds from the neighboring houses into the loft and basement, and we got some of the fencing done to adjoin both houses. I'm hoping we will manage to finish the fencing before the others come."

"So you finally believe me, eh, Mike?" I asked.

"Yes, I do," Mike responded matter-of-factly. "The Holy Spirit confirmed it."

"Okay," Tim said, "the sun is setting, and we need to get moving again. Tell Ruby and John we said hi and we love them."

"I will," Mike said. "We will pray for your safety. Bye." He clicked off the walkie.

A few minutes later, we left the cabin. We headed in the direction of the lavender farm until the woods became so dark that we needed our night-vision goggles. The stars shone brightly this far north of the major cities. If we hadn't been injured, it would have been a joy to travel. Fire perked up a bit and ran ahead of us several times.

After many hours, Tim's breath became labored, and I asked, "Do you need to take another break?"

"No, we need to press on. I'd like to find Ruth before winter," Tim explained, continuing into a clearing in the middle of the woods.

"Stop right where you are!" a voice shouted, and bright lights shone all around us, blinding us and causing Fire to whimper and cower behind me.

Oh no, not again, I thought.

Printed in the United States
by Baker & Taylor Publisher Services